The Crushing of Wild Mint

The Crushing of Wild Mint

Diane Tate

WestBow
PRESS
A DIVISION OF THOMAS NELSON

Copyright © 2012 Diane Tate

All rights reserved. No part of this book may be used or reproduced by any means, graphic, electronic, or mechanical, including photocopying, recording, taping or by any information storage retrieval system without the written permission of the publisher except in the case of brief quotations embodied in critical articles and reviews.

ISBN: 978-1-4497-5373-3 (e)
ISBN: 978-1-4497-5377-1 (sc)
ISBN: 978-1-4497-5376-4 (hc)

Library of Congress Control Number: 2012909175

WestBow Press books may be ordered through booksellers or by contacting:

WestBow Press
A Division of Thomas Nelson
1663 Liberty Drive
Bloomington, IN 47403
www.westbowpress.com
1-(866) 928-1240

Because of the dynamic nature of the Internet, any web addresses or links contained in this book may have changed since publication and may no longer be valid. The views expressed in this work are solely those of the author and do not necessarily reflect the views of the publisher, and the publisher hereby disclaims any responsibility for them.

Any people depicted in stock imagery provided by Thinkstock are models, and such images are being used for illustrative purposes only.
Certain stock imagery © Thinkstock.

Scripture taken from the King James Version of the Bible.

Printed in the United States of America

WestBow Press rev. date: 6/29/2012

In loving memory of

Philip

My very own "Billy Russell"

CONTENTS

"OF LEAF AND FLOWER"	ix
1. THE STORYTELLER	1
2. RUN	5
3. IN THE TOWN WHERE NOTHING HAPPENS	7
4. HUMBLE BEGINNINGS	15
5. BIRTHDAY GIRL	22
6. ALOES AND PRICKLES	25
7. HERITAGE	31
8. JOHN PRUITT WALLACE	37
9. PARTY TIME	43
10. A DOG'S LIFE	49
11. COOL AS MINT	52
12. BACK TO THE PARTY	54
13. JUGGLING	60
14. GENTLEMAN FARMER	64
15. ROSE SATIN	67
16. GUESTS?	72
17. SMALL KINGDOM	76
18. BANKER'S HOURS	78
19. HEADS UP, JO	80
20. BANKER BLUES	84
21. NEVER ASK	86
22. LITTLE BROTHER	93
23. BREAKDOWN	96
24. BEST FRIENDS	99

25. SEARCH	103
26. SECOND GUESSING	119
27. TRIAGE	122
28. TAKE CARE OF IT!	126
29. EPIPHANY	134
30. MORE ANSWERS	136
31. PLANS	147
32. SMOKEHOUSE SEASONING	151
33. TRUST ME	153
34. EXCURSIONS	163
35. TRUTH	198
36. REAL SOUTHERN, REAL GOOD!	206
37. BILLY RUSSELL GOES TO THE DOGS	219
38. THE DEAL	239
39. WEDDING PREP	242
40. BITTERSWEET	252
41. JUST SAY GOODNIGHT	258
42. WAKE UP AND GO TO BED!	263
EPILOGUE	269

"OF LEAF AND FLOWER"

Sturdy trees,

Both great and small,

Protect lesser plants

And give shade to all,

A quiet place to rest.

Their roots are sure

And go deep,

Great strength

In their bending.

The smallest,

Palest blossom fair,

Her nectar ever drawing;

Alluring color,

A flush to skin,

Birds and bees

Go deep within,

Seemingly inconsequential—

Until she springs with life.

D. L.T.

ACKNOWLEDGMENTS

Special thanks to Debra, Melody, and Darlene

Also

Anita, Rose Anne, and Patti

And

My dear brothers, Steve and Paul, and your precious families

Finally

Jim, Bill, and Joanne

Thank you for all the prayers, love and encouragement.

1. THE STORYTELLER

The old woman slipped out early to the waiting back porch, careful of the screen door, as its usual screeching would awaken her husband. The sun was not up yet, but it was daylight. The sky was just beginning to break the first faint streaks of color, suggesting the urgency of the day. A mocking bird's shrill cry disquieted her, shaking away the last traces of sleep. In the distance, she could hear the sound of the mourning dove, its call soft, almost a coo. Everything else was quiet.

This time of morning was always special, the air still fresh. Though the dew covered the grass in heavy droplets, the sun would make short work of it. A new day had begun and with it came possibilities.

She would sit for a moment and drink in the quiet stillness until the delicious aroma of the coffee awakened her senses. There was absolutely nothing better than that first cup, well—maybe one thing, maybe iced tea with a sprig of fresh mint. No matter. She would get to that later.

She had many plans for the day. Slowly her mind began to focus on the needs of her gardens. She would pull weeds and move a few of the younger, sturdier plants. This would give them room to spread, a place to become the size and shape they were meant to be.

The early crop of green beans had filled out and was ready. She should get to those about mid-morning. The dew would be off by then.

A few more sips from her favorite cup and she would begin. After that, she would put on her well-worn gardening shoes and lace them up, a habit she had learned from her father. He would always go to the porch barefooted in warm weather and put his shoes on there before he went out for the day. He did this to keep his footsteps from waking the family. How she had loved her father; he was such a sweet memory. *Later,* she thought.

The first rays of sun eased over the tree line, and she knew it was time. She picked up her basket, always sure to find something ripe or a flower ready, and stepped off the porch into the lush, wet foliage of her flower garden. Dee Dee, a descendant of the original family cat, went with her, always ready to pounce on anything that moved. This cat was still young and playful, hungry for imagined adventure.

The Crushing of Wild Mint

The woman pulled stray plants and creeping vines from between the roses and continued to wake up. Activity always helped with this process. She loved the way gardening of any kind seemed to work on the mind as well as the body. Though old now, her muscles were strong and her joints moved freely in spite of stiffness at times. But more than that, gardening released her mind, and her thoughts came more freely. Only random thoughts would come at first, but slowly, the thoughts came together allowing her to make sense of most things.

She stood while brushing dirt from her faded blue skirt and wiping her hands on the apron. Looking around, she was quite satisfied. The garden had come alive in the last week; it happened that way every year. Early summer was one of her favorite seasons.

Her basket was full now, and it was time to go to the shade of the porch. Though it was still early, the combination of heavy dew and sunshine made the air quite heavy. She sat in her chair, removed her hat, and began fanning herself with it. She poured the first glass of iced tea for the day. *Yes, a sprig of mint would be nice*, she thought as she took a sip. Sifting through the basket of just picked blossoms, she found a young, green sprig. As she brushed a leaf, it released a bit of its delicate scent. With the mint in her glass, she sipped again. *That is much better*, she decided. It was more an event of aroma than of taste.

She sat there, rocking, cooling from the heat of the morning, and drinking the tea. The creaking of the old, weathered chair gave evidence to its use and age. The lemony-sweet taste of the tea and the smell of the mint brought back old memories. In her mind's eye, she could see everything as clearly as though it were yesterday.

2. RUN

Mason had to keep going! His mind and his lungs were screaming, *Faster, faster, jump!*

He was so tired of trying to make the next train out of town before railroad agents could catch him. For what seemed a very long time now, all he could remember was running as hard and as fast as he could. He no longer had a choice. It was run, prison, or die.

At fifteen, he had left the current shack of a house his parents called home. He had been so sure there was an easier way of life than picking cotton. Mason had seen his daddy work as hard as any draft horse or mule, but they had nothing to show for it. Their lives had been about scrimping, just getting by, and doing without.

Yes, he knew his current way of life was wrong. It didn't matter. He was not going back to that! But what was he going to do? At the age of forty-two, he couldn't keep doing this. His aching body told him that much. Though hardened by rough living, he had lost the will to keep going. It was just too hard! He had barely caught this train. Old injuries were constant reminders of schemes that had gone awry.

Common sense told him more than once he should part company with his two present running mates. One was sick—disgusting; the other one was crazy. Mason didn't know which was worse.

He had run with others, and he had run farther than most. It was all the same in the end—they ran until they got caught or died

He needed time to think, and sleep, if he could just close his weary eyes for a few minutes. They were safe for now. "Sick" and "Crazy" were already in the box car.

The smoke-billowing train was in full throttle and wasn't due to stop for several hours. The rhythmic motion of the swaying cars and the music of the tracks would be enough to dull the senses, ease the body, and lull the mind into blessed unconsciousness. They would hear and feel the train slowing and wake up just in time to jump off before it stopped—or they wouldn't. Right now, he didn't care. He could not think anymore.

Tired to the bone, hungry, and aching, Mason slept the sleep of the dead.

3. IN THE TOWN WHERE NOTHING HAPPENS

When a place is dormant for a very long time, certain conditions come together to create a vacuum. Out of that vacuum comes a fully blown storm.

It could have been any small, rural town in the early 1900's. It was the kind of place where nothing ever happens, except on this particular Friday night, something did.

The train station was unusually crowded. Three or four men waited on the wooden benches outside the small telegraph office. It was very warm. Windows and doors stood open wide to catch any breeze however brief. A few nervous women and over-tired children were milling about, trying to find lodging for the night and transportation out of town the next day. Everyone's plans had changed. The train had made an unexpected stop due to heavy rain that had washed out the tracks about two miles out of town. It would take at least a week to re-lay the track, but first, gandy dancers, old timers, and other workers, would have to be brought in from Nashville. There were certain advantages to living near the Tennessee-Alabama border, but remoteness was not one of them.

"Boy," called the telegrapher. "Come in here. I've a message that needs deliverin'. It's a 'might important too. Go tell the bank manager he's got a deposit to pick up today. Hurry, it'll be almost closin' time. Give him this here telegram."

The messenger boy smiled sweetly and doffed his father's oversized cap to Mr. Percy, knowing the telegrapher would put a penny in it for his trouble. He took the message and off he ran as fast as his young, bare feet would carry him. Charlie liked running errands. It made him feel grown up. He was especially happy when someone gave him a penny.

Being a sweet, simple, unassuming youth, people often said things they shouldn't in his presence. This was good because Charlie soon found the true character of people, those whom he could trust, and those he could not.

Charlie ran down Depot Street, straight to the bank. He found the manager and handed him the telegram. It read:

To Whom It May Concern STOP

The train tracks have washed out below your town STOP On the train is $50,000.00 enroute to our station in Birmingham for the steel industry STOP It will be at least a week before the track is fixed STOP The rail line would consider it a professional courtesy if you would receive the deposit and lock it in your bank's vault until the train can continue or one of our agents can be sent to retrieve the money STOP Please advise as to the feasibility of this plan STOP You have our deepest gratitude in the matter STOP

Sincerely,

Hayden Farris, Farris Rail Line

John Vernon Wallace, the bank manager, who everyone just called Wallace, thought a moment, considered the situation, reached in his pocket, and removed three pennies.

"Charlie, I need you to do some running for me. First, go down to my house, find my wife, and tell her I'm going to be late tonight. We're supposed to go to a party, so please tell her to go to the party without me. I'll be along later. Then, go directly back to the telegraph station and give Mr. Percy this reply to be sent to the rail line's office. Can you remember all of that, Charlie?"

"Yes, sir, I can!" replied the young boy.

"Well then, here's a penny for speaking to my wife, a penny for getting back to the telegraph office quickly, and a penny for delivering my note. And thank you, Charlie."

Charlie ran immediately to do as he was asked. Everyone knew him to be a very reliable child, and this too, made him happy.

He tried his best to be a good boy, and he hoped to someday be a good man. He could hear his mama's words, "Charlie, always do what's right, and one day you will be a very good man. And Charlie, your mama loves you. Be good." And he was.

Charlie found Mrs. Wallace, delivered the message, and ran back to the telegraph station with the reply to be sent to the rail line. It simply acknowledged their request, stated the matter would be attended as requested, and signed Vernon Wallace, Bank Manager.

Charlie had done very well today. He was satisfied.

Mr. Wallace considered what he should do first. He realized he should stop by the jail and explain the situation to the town constable. He would ask him to both witness the pickup of the money and act as security if needed. The event of that happening was highly unlikely in this town.

Henry Milton, the town constable, was an easy going man. This could be an asset in an explosive situation. So far, he had never had to do more than break up fights between friends when they got drunk.

The constable had been a school teacher up north for many years.

He soon realized if a desire to learn was not present in a child, only rudimentary facts could be taught. Those facts were basically what the public wanted, but Milton had wanted to teach much more.

It seemed to Henry there was always so much more to learn about the sciences, the laws which seemingly ruled the Universe, and he believed those disciplines contained the secrets of life. He was continually amazed with the way the world was a self-sustaining cycle run by smaller cycles within, ever renewing the whole thing. And numbers, he often lost track of time while contemplating the relationships among numbers. He believed an equation could be written for almost every situation in life. Unfortunately, most people seemed more interested in making money and enjoying ball games than actually understanding how they fit into the beautiful, physical world around them. Apathy from the public in general had taken its toll on the teacher.

When Henry read about a small town needing law and order, he decided to go south and try a career change. It had worked. People trusted him, and it was not as if he ever had to fight a crime wave or deal with any real hostility.

Wallace and the constable went to the telegraph office first to make sure the telegram of assurance had been sent to the rail line. It had. Next, they found the train's security officer, got the money from the safe, and counted it. They each signed a receipt for the amount.

A few minutes later, Mr. Wallace unlocked the door of the bank.

Though small, it was furnished with a beautiful, thick, emerald green carpet that was trimmed in a broad, gold leaf pattern around the edge. There was a small entry in front of the lone booth, and behind that, there stood an oak, roll top desk where Mr. Wallace worked, and the safe. It was simple but adequate for a town of this size.

Wallace and the constable brought the money to the back of the teller's booth. The manager took a small key from his pocket, unlocked the roll top desk, opened a drawer, and lifted a false bottom from the drawer. He put both his copy of the receipt for the money and the telegram he had received into the drawer and replaced the false bottom. He did not want to leave any evidence of the deposit where it could easily be seen. Wallace locked the desk and slipped the key back into his pocket.

He went to the safe with the bag of money, unlocked it with the combination, put the money inside, and shut the door. He turned to leave and remembered something. Sometimes, the thick, safe door did not align as it should and would need a nudge. As he shouldered the door and pushed, Wallace listened for the "click" that assured him the lock had engaged.

After seeing the money had been securely put away, the constable was anxious to begin his nightly rounds of the rural town, making sure all was well and as it should be.

"Wallace, it seems we're finished here, so I'll be heading out," he stated.

As Milton put on his hat the banker replied, "Thank you, Henry, for your time and help. Will I see you later at the party?"

"I wouldn't miss it!" After saying that, the constable left.

The cautious banker took one more look around. Satisfied everything was secure, he, too, headed for home.

Though he was running late, he decided to take time to wash up a bit and change clothes. A fresh shirt and nicer suit would be more appropriate. Besides, his socially prominent wife would fuss if he didn't put forth the effort to dress for the occasion. The whole town had been invited, and it should be a very nice event. It wasn't every day that the girl next door, the beautiful daughter of dear friends, celebrated her twenty-first birthday.

It was a very short drive to his home, just to the edge of town. He went into the study, unloaded his pockets, and stopped. The key to the roll top desk was not there. He retraced his steps to the car and searched the ground but found nothing. Reasoning he was already late for the party and a few minutes more would not matter, he drove back to town thinking he might have lost it in front of the bank.

After lighting the lantern he carried in the car for emergencies, he searched the ground and steps to the bank, but found nothing there either. He tried the door. It was still locked. *Good,* he thought. Looking through the front window, he could see nothing on the floor. He reasoned that if he could see nothing with a lantern, then no one else could either. Probably, in the light of day, the key would be found. Besides, it was just the key to the desk, not the front door.

He continued to look as he went back to the car. Wallace had done all he could for now. He would just get up early tomorrow and find the key. No one else needed to know.

He was really going to be late for the party now. Mrs. Wallace would be upset with him.

4. HUMBLE BEGINNINGS

Every town, especially a rural town, needs a doctor. This small, pastoral community was no different. They not only had a good doctor, but the good doctor was also a good man.

Samuel Harrison Windham knew he had been blessed. He counted those blessings every time he looked at his family. He gave thanks for his beautiful wife, Vivian, two daughters, and a son who were now young adults. He had friends who were actually good people and a successful medical practice. At forty-seven, he was quite satisfied with his life. It had not begun that way.

Harrison had been born in a time unlike any other in America's history, the few years before the Civil War. He had lived through the war and witnessed those hardships and the succeeding time of poverty and hunger.

The years that followed the war seemed excessively cruel to the South, for they had lost a lot more than the war. Generations of fathers and sons had been lost, and the men who came home returned to a world they did not know.

When Harrison was very young, his father, Joseph Harrison Windham, had gone to fight for the Confederacy. Just surviving the moment to moment struggles of the war had been a miracle in itself. The harshness of the war continued as he returned to Tennessee, only to find the place he had left was no more.

Before the war, his family had owned a small farm. It was enough to meet their needs, and they had been happy.

At some point during the war, their cattle had been slaughtered to feed one of the armies. Looters took what was left and burned the home. The land grew rough and uncultivated, overgrown with brush and thistle. But worse than that, the ground had been seized for back taxes and sold on the steps of the court house. The Windham land had been bought by a profiteer for pennies on the dollar and resold. It was all gone now. They would have to start over.

Like the Windhams, there were many other families who had lost their lands and possessions. Farms that would have been an inheritance for generations had been destroyed and taken over by anyone with a purse large enough to rebuild and work the ground.

Joseph did not have time to grieve over the loss of his land; he needed to take care of his family. He knew farming, so he hired on as a sharecropper where ever he could find work. With so many families in this situation, they had to move around a lot.

Harrison's father worked very long days, but in spite of this, they often found themselves in a one room shack that was not much more than four walls, a roof, and dirt floor. At times, they were evicted even from that.

There was, usually, something to eat because his mama had deadly aim with a rifle. The woods and fields provided a supply of rabbit and squirrel, but there wasn't much else. In the spring of the year, she would go to the woods and scout for the young, green shoots of the pokeweed. The greens were good tasting and safe to eat if boiled twice, the water drained after each cooking, then scrambled with eggs. To make that meal work, his mother needed to have a piece of side meat, pork slices fried crispy. She had side meat only if the landowner gave her a piece because he owned the hogs. According to Harrison's parents and prevailing folklore, poke salad greens and side meat should be eaten with water bread—crusty, doughy pone made from a white cornmeal without any rising agent and water, nothing else. In late June after the potatoes had been dug, landowners would give them some of the crop. Later, the seasons brought sweet potatoes and turnip greens that tasted better after the first frost, again, according to folklore.

Harrison would have had siblings. Two brothers were stillborn, and a sister had died at an early age from tuberculosis. Mortality rates were high for the very young in the post Civil War era due to the prevailing poverty of the day and the lack of modern medical discoveries.

The Windhams did whatever they had to do to survive. Eventually, time and opportunity happened to all who worked and took advantage of the choices offered to them. The South was rebuilt, and with that came new opportunities for growth. People moved on with their lives. New fortunes were made, and other careers were explored. In general, people adjusted to fortune and misfortune as it occurred.

Harrison promised himself that someday he would become a doctor. He had seen enough suffering. He worked at every part-time job he could find, saved his money, and got through medical school. He knew it was worth the struggle when he set the broken bones of a logger, his first patient. The man would walk straight again, be able to care for his family, because he, Harrison Windham, had become a very good doctor.

Then he met Vivian. Vivian Morton was slender and auburn haired, an absolute beauty, a daughter of wealth and position. He had known her for two weeks when he proposed.

Vivian immediately saw in Harrison, kindness, intelligence, and wisdom. These were lasting qualities that would only bring honor to an already honorable man. She loved him too.

Her parents would not hear of it of course, but young love is a powerfully impulsive thing. They eloped!

Leaving early one morning to find a Justice of the Peace, they married and came home two days later. When the young couple returned, Vivian's parents simply said, "What was done was done." They realized they should all just make the best of it. Besides, Vivian had always been a strong-willed girl, and her parents knew arguing would get them nowhere. Neither did they want a scandal.

The Mortons actually liked Harrison. Vivian should make a good life with him. This marriage would not be the social, financial merger they had hoped for, but there was considerable status to being the wife of a well respected doctor, and they reasoned, they had more than enough resources for two lifetimes.

Harrison and Vivian were very happy while it was just the two of them, and it got even better when they learned they were to have their first child, a little boy, Samuel Harrison Windham, Junior. That was the happiest day of Harrison's life.

The saddest day was the day they buried the child. It was no one's fault, but the young parents blamed themselves anyway. Sam Jr. had just gotten over measles and a slight cold the week before. He seemed completely well—only a few spots remained. The child had been eating well, playing, happy. There were no signs of complications. He simply slipped away in the night.

The burden of grief is hard enough to bear, but the demon of guilt haunts and torments until there is nothing left. It was tragic irony for Harrison. He was a skilled doctor with mastery of the sciences and medicine, but he could not save his own son. He had cared for others, watched over them in their most critical moments, but all of his skill and experience could not foresee things hidden by a robust countenance.

Harrison seemed much older after the loss, and he would never be the same. There was melancholy about him, sadness—always just a bit withdrawn.

Vivian was drowning in her own sadness. She could not be reached on any level for a very long time. She would not be comforted.

Though she truly never *blamed* Harrison, and would never voice the question, she could not help but wonder how he had missed this.

Life can be so good at the most unexpected times, and as fate would have it, eventually a baby girl was born to them. Harrison came alive again because he thought the sun arose in the little girl's smile.

Miriam Adelicia Windham, Mary Alice, grew into a fair, delicate beauty. She was slender like her mother, but had blond hair and blue-green eyes that were like the color of the sea.

Harrison doted on Mary Alice. He rushed home to see her every day, tucked her in every night, and held her close through every storm.

Vivian was a loving mother who insisted on doing everything perfectly for the child. She was a devoted parent as well.

Harrison could not put his finger on the slight change he had seen in Vivian. She was still beautiful, a wonderful wife, and mother. Certainly, Mary Alice had brought them great joy, but she would never erase the loss they felt for Sam Jr. Maybe that was what he saw in Vivian.

The birth of their second daughter two years later, brought them Josephine Clarice, and two years after that, another son, William Russell. Vivian insisted on giving all of their children proper Christian names. The only child who retained that formality was Josephine, who grew to be exactly like her mother. Though very pretty, the girl rarely smiled.

Harrison loved all of his children, but as they grew, a special bond developed with Alice. Josephine usually aligned herself with Vivian, and Billy Russell, being an audacious, fun loving boy, was usually in the middle, like a puppy—ripping, tearing, and teasing everyone.

Today was Mary Alice's twenty-first birthday, and later, there would be a wonderful party. People, friends really, would come to the Windham home to celebrate. Again Harrison would count his many blessings.

5. BIRTHDAY GIRL

Petey awoke with a start. His little heart was racing. That smell—he knew there was a cat very near. He could barely see light an inch or two wide through the cloth that enveloped his cage. Someone had left the bedroom door open, and Delilah had eased through with the stealth of a viper.

He had been through this before. That awful cat would pounce on his cage, swinging it until it fell. Then she would twist her body and reach through the bars until her claws had him.

Petey knew Delilah was getting close. A cat hair floated past him. He trembled! *He must awaken Mary Alice. She would save him; she loved him. She needed him! How many times had she told him? He was the only one who really understood her.*

Panic mode set in! Instantly, he began to flap his wings against the bars, stir and shake the cage for everything he was worth. He could be very vocal too, and now was the time!

Mary Alice also awoke with a start! It was very difficult to sleep with a small war in the room. She immediately knew what was happening, raced for the cat, threw her into the hall, and shut the door.

Turning to her pet, Mary Alice cooed, "Poor Petey, has Josephine's nasty cat got you rattled?"

She righted his cage as Petey stopped flapping his little, blue wings and flitted to his perch. Clinging there, he visibly breathed a sigh of relief, and his heart began to slow into a gentler rhythm. He cautiously looked around the room. As he did so, his chatter slowly became a song.

Mary Alice went back to snuggle in the warmth of her bed, still talking gently to Petey, trying to soothe the bird.

She suddenly realized it was her birthday. She was twenty-one, an adult. A slow smile crept across her face until it was a huge grin. This day had been a long time in coming. Tonight, there would be a party, and she meant to enjoy herself!

Vivian Morton Windham had already started a campaign to get both Mary Alice and Josephine married. She felt a mother could not begin too early when considering suitable husband material for her daughters.

Vivian had made it very clear, "It's time you were taking men seriously, Mary Alice. You must consider someone for marriage."

Vivian could hear the voice of her own mother saying the same words some twenty-five years earlier. She had rolled her eyes and had shaken her head then, just as Alice was doing now.

Well, Mary Alice intended to make her mother happy. She also wanted to make Everett McKenzie "happy" tonight. He had said they needed time to grow up. She intended to give him that. She would dance and flirt with every male at her party. She would make them both very happy!

Alice yawned and stretched in her bed, savoring the last few minutes of "nothingness." *Everett,* she thought with a sigh. *Did he need more time than the three years he had been away?* She hoped not.

She could only know her own heart. If he did not love her—she needed to move on.

Realizing this made her somewhat anxious. She knew the bliss of sleeping-in was over. She rolled out of bed, uncovered Petey's cage, and asked, "Well, shall we begin?"

As if in reply, he fluffed some feathers, preened a bit, and began his morning song.

6. ALOES AND PRICKLES

The old woman stirred a bit in her chair, a little confused from her surroundings. Memories of children had alerted her consciousness. She had not meant to fall asleep. It was early yet, and there was still much to do.

She rolled down the sleeves of her shirt and pulled on her gloves. There were so many delicious things in the garden, but their leaves would make her itch harshly when they touched her skin. She would step into the vegetable garden and see if the corn was ready. She could already taste sweet corn and tomatoes with bacon from the smokehouse. Too bad, it wasn't ready. In another two to three days, the kernels would be full of milk instead of the water they now held.

She would check the okra next. There were only a few pods mature enough to cook and these were sternly clinging to stalks under broad, prickly leaves. Ever prepared, she had placed a small knife in her basket. Using the knife, she clipped the pods and moved on to the squash. One never knew about squash. One day it was ready, another day, overripe. It was either food or seed.

Turning to go back to the porch, she stepped in a patch of wild mint, the fragrance instantly cooling. Though she had planted peppermint beside her other herbs, a garnish for many recipes, the wild mint always smelled just as wonderful.

The woman sat again and began fanning herself with her hat. Still uneasy from the heat, she rolled up her sleeves to get some air and pulled up the skirt of her apron to wipe her brow. She poured more tea and drank deeply before she started the task of breaking the early green beans.

As she began to cool, she thought about the smell of the mint. Plants were truly remarkable. They were different, like people. Aloe, for instance, could heal.

She immediately thought of Corinne Fitzpatrick, her neighbor of more than twenty years and her dearest friend. One of the most beautiful memories of the old woman's life had come through tragedy and grief. Corinne had displayed the gift of compassion at a time when it was desperately needed.

The old woman's heart had been broken, her soul crushed. She felt she was somehow at fault for what had happened. There was no one else she would dare blame. Time had eased some of the pain, or maybe, now she was just stronger. Too, other joys had moved into her soul, filling some of the deserted places with new life.

Corinne had come over late that day. She already knew the sadness of the situation. Finding the woman on her bed, Corinne's heart broke fresh for her friend. As Corinne's tears fell and ran the length of her arm, so too had the woman's tears fallen, running together, joining in a common pool of sorrow. Corinne knew words were not important at a time like this, but friendship, sharing a burden with someone, was everything.

Corinne sat with the woman allowing her grief to purge. As she brushed back the hair from the woman's tear streaked face she asked, "Do you think you could just sit up and drink a little water?"

The woman made no reply but sat up, leaning on Corinne, weeping in silence. Corinne was patient. She held the woman for a moment then helped her into a bedside chair. She wiped the tears from her face and put a glass of water to the woman's lips. She managed to sip a little. Corinne believed it would be good if her friend could just sit up a while, so in hushed tones she asked, "Do you think you could just sit here a few minutes? Your pillow is soaked. Let me change the bedding. I promise I'll be quick. Fresh sheets will help you rest."

Ah, the magic word. The word she had not considered in many days, "rest". Would she ever have rest again? It seemed doubtful.

The woman did not really care what Corinne did or said. She was numb and waiting for death to bring "rest". It seemed unimportant whether she waited for it on clean or dirty sheets.

Strangely though, she realized she could actually breathe better sitting up, and, like Corinne had said, maybe cool sheets would help in the waiting. The coolness might sooth the burning hollows of her eyes. The swelling of her face might shrink, and maybe, she could just go to sleep as the child had done.

"Yes, Corinne, I'll sit here, and thank you."

Corinne went about cleaning, taking her time changing the bed linens. When finished, she turned back the covers, plumped the pillows, and sprayed some lavender into the air.

The bed looked so inviting to the woman. She looked at her bedraggled nightgown and then at Corinne. "I'm a mess," she conceded.

"We can fix that too," Corinne volunteered softly.

She went to the bureau and found a gown of soft batiste. Next, she gathered some toilet articles and helped her with a bath. After helping her get dressed, Corinne gently brushed the woman's hair until it was shiny and smooth against the woman's back.

Helping her into bed, Corinne asked, "Did you say the doctor left something to help you sleep? This would be a good time to take it. You must rest—a little while anyway."

The woman took the potion. Escape for just a little while from the crushing thoughts seemed like a good idea. There would always be tomorrow to remember. If not, she would be with her little Sam. Hot, fresh tears ran now.

The next day, Corinne brought flowers for the woman's bedroom, their scent clean and sweet. Every day she came over to help her wounded friend, helping her to drink a little broth and patiently coaxing her to live. Slowly, the woman grew stronger, stayed up a little longer, and began to look forward to her friend's visits.

By the end of the second week Corinne brought the woman a gift. "Come outside," she said. "See what I've brought you." There on the patio, was a yellow rose bush, ready to be planted.

"Do you think you could help me plant the rose—in memory of the child?" Corinne asked.

Tears came quickly to the woman's eyes, but these were tears of love and gratitude. Corinne had done so much for her. She could never repay her kindness. The woman would never get over the loss of the child, but now she would focus on the beauty of his life in the renewed beauty of the rose every year and the love of a dear friend.

The old woman came back to the present then, her eyes wet as usual from the pain and the beauty of the memory. The yellow rose bush had been only the beginning of her garden. She had tended and cared for the rose as though it had been a newborn. Gradually she added other plants to the garden spot until it had grown to its present size. Later, she had added a small patch of vegetables. That too had grown.

She found gardening made her strong, not only physically, but mentally and spiritually as well.

Gardening released her mind to consider possibilities to things; she gleaned truth from fancy. Through the years she found great comfort too, confessing worries and fears, releasing them, committing their resolution to God through prayer.

She fondly considered her other neighbors then, her dear friends the McKenzies and the Wallaces. They too had become as family. The occasion had begun with joy but ended quite differently. She began to remember Mary Alice's twenty-first birthday and the awful weekend that followed.

7. HERITAGE

The ground that was found north of the small community was a bit rough, thin soil over limestone in most places. The vegetation could only be described as scrub brush and scraggly cedar trees, but to the south, a man could find thick, rich, dark dirt. It was the kind of nutrient rich soil that yielded heavy harvests, soil that was everything a farmer could want.

Maxwell and Irene McKenzie did not have a large farm by some standards, but it was all theirs. They owned two hundred acres of the finest ground anywhere. There were gently rolling hills for pasture, three, spring fed ponds, a creek with fertile bottom ground for crops, and woodlands.

Maxwell, with the help of his father, Tillman, and his son, Everett, stayed busy year round, plowing, planting, harvesting or hauling something somewhere.

"Miss Irene" took care of the house, garden, dairy cattle, and fowl. They were a very close family, and each enjoyed a feeling of accomplishment at the end of the day.

Jupiter was Miss Irene's dog, a traditional black and white border collie, mostly black from nose to tail, white underneath from muzzle to chest with a mass of white through the ruff of his neck. He was truly a beautiful, intelligent dog with a tolerant disposition and boundless energy. He, well he and Miss Irene actually, ran the place.

Jupiter's purpose in life was to responsibly herd the dairy cattle in his care and watch over his family. He would protect them with his life if needed. The collie enjoyed working with Miss Irene and loved the feel of her gentle hands in praise of his good work.

He also loved Everett, almost as much as his mistress. Jupiter was overjoyed now that Everett was home to stay. It had been a long three years for his people. He had heard Everett's name mentioned in every prayer offered.

Maxwell and Irene McKenzie were ordinary people, but she was a woman of faith, and he was a man of prayer. Because of this, they never felt alone though they had the same struggles, burdens, and conflicts as everyone else.

Maxwell had been truly blessed in so many ways that he could not count them all, but he tried. Every day he prayed, thanking God for each of his loved ones. He had a noble dog that kept watch over the finest farm in the county; a grown son who was honest, kind and intelligent in all of his dealings; a beautiful, faithful wife who believed in him, and he still had his own father, the man who had taught him everything he knew.

Maxwell was truly grateful for his blessings, but more than these, one more and the greatest of all, he walked daily with his God, and this gave him peace.

There were times, especially in the evenings, when Maxwell could sense God's presence so real that he could almost visualize another soul by his side, listening to every burden and care he had ever borne. In farming there would always be an unknown factor to cause concern. Weather, sickness in livestock, and accidents would always be concerns; the list was always there. The one constant had always been an ever abiding presence; the still small voice that guided Maxwell's every decision.

Though Maxwell had also depended on his son, he felt the young man needed to grow up in many ways. To do so, Everett was sent east to study the latest in farming practices, machinery, and veterinary medicine. During the three years Everett had been away, Maxwell had hired drifters, sharecroppers, and anyone else he could find to fill the gap. The long wait was over now. Everett had left the farm as a skilled, hard working youth, but he returned as a young man, wise and capable in every way.

Everett McKenzie was very glad to be home. He had known the farm would be his someday, and he needed to learn everything he could about farming improvements in order to make it an even more productive business. He hated to leave his family with all the work, but everyone knew it would be for the best in the long run.

Also, he had not wanted to leave Mary Alice, but knew she needed the time to mature. She needed to know her own mind and heart. If she was sure of "forever," then he was ready to commit.

He had just gotten home the day before and learned they were all invited to the Windham's home for Mary Alice's birthday party.

Mary Alice. He had thought of her every day. Had she thought of him? There was something in the way she had looked at him at their last meeting that made him believe she would.

Everett remembered fondly how as children they had all played together either on his farm, the big back yard at the Windham's, or at the lake on the Benton's land.

When they were very young, they played in the grove of trees between the houses. Their mothers ever diligent, watching them from the windows to be sure they were still there and safe.

The mothers did not know however, in the course of time, brush and young trees had grown around an open area in the middle of the grove. It was not visible until you were actually at the stand of trees. This was where Alice, Geri and Avery went to get away from Billy Russell, Alice's baby brother. It was where Everett found Josephine trying to kiss John Wallace. And, this was where he had found Mary Alice, having cried herself to sleep because he had not come to her birthday party. Everett had sat beside the sleeping girl and recited from a poem, "As long as the rain falls / and as surely as a Whippoorwill calls / I will always love you, Mary Alice." She was twelve, he fifteen.

He had wanted to go to the party, but the rain was coming fast. His family was going to lose the hay if they could not get it in the barn.

Even at fifteen he was sure he was in love with her. At that age he might not know a lot about love, but he knew about a racing heart, clammy hands, and not being able to think coherently when they were together.

He checked the inside pocket of his dinner jacket to make sure he had not forgotten her gift. The small box was there, neatly wrapped in blue, paisley paper and ribbon. Inside, was the same pearl choker he had planned to give her nine years ago at her twelfth birthday. He had added another strand of perfectly matched pearls and an aquamarine stone. She had always loved the blue-green color of the stone because it seemed exotic to her.

While he was in East Tennessee studying, he had gone to the Atlantic shoreline for a few days to enjoy a break. He had never seen the ocean. The powerfully surging waves were beyond imagination. The color of the frothy water was the same gray, blue-green as Alice's eyes, and he had thought of her. As he walked along the wet sand, wishing she could be there to see it with him, he stepped on what he thought was just a rock. It had turned out to be an aquamarine, the perfect stone for her necklace.

He could already see how she would look when she opened the box. The anticipation he felt for giving the gift was sweet, but there was more. Everett knew he was in love with her. Mary Alice would not cry herself to sleep tonight! This birthday would be different.

8. JOHN PRUITT WALLACE

Ethical standards are different for all of us. We give evidence of our true character, both good and bad, every day. We may not be able to see who we are, but others can.

John Pruitt Wallace thought himself quite handsome as he checked his appearance in the hall mirror. His suit was expensive, his shoes were shiny, and he felt very confident about the evening ahead.

Though he possessed a personality that was genuine and likeable, it was usually masked by his interest in creating and executing deals that were to his advantage. Though most deals were basically the same, the outcome is equal to the objective minus the challenges, he found each deal unique in the way people could be manipulated and circumstances molded to suit the desires others.

Unfortunately, his attitude about business carried over into his personal relationships, and he sometimes found it difficult to separate the two. John thought the best way to deal with women was to flirt with them, make them feel special. That was not hard to do. Women were easily led, and he could usually find something pleasant to say and be sincere about it. Men, on the other hand, needed to be enticed by some reward or threatened by a show of power. He had not developed these attitudes over night.

John's parents were good people, but their lives were about social connections, monetary gain, and control. They thought they had taught John all the important lessons of life. He knew how to set up a deal, manipulate the principal players, and apply a little pressure if needed. In short, how to get exactly what he wanted.

His mother was a prominent socialite, his father, the local banker. Because of these circumstances, John had been provided ample opportunity to hone his skill into seamless art. You simply never saw what was coming until John was closing the deal, and there was no way out.

There was no *need* for John to have this attitude about people. He had been blessed with friends who were honestly good people. Neighbors who went to church every Sunday, said grace before meals, and took care of you when you were sick. He knew them all very well.

As children, they usually got along and seldom got into trouble because there was always someone watching them from one house or another. John was two years older than Alice, Geri and Avery. He usually got his way, so sometimes the three younger simply did not ask him to play with them. There was Billy Russell, Alice's baby brother, and Josephine, Alice's sister, whom they could hardly abide. She was the tattle-tale and had to do everything perfectly. She was no fun! There was also Everett, the McKenzie's son, who was older still than John. The children really liked Everett, but he couldn't always play because there was usually something on his farm that needed urgent attention.

They were all grown up now. John Wallace did not consider himself to have a real best friend. He had become too much of a rogue for that. Most men were jealous of his money, power, and the way he had with women. He could not help himself; whenever he met a man or a woman, he systematically filed them into categories for future reference and possible use.

The women in his life were his mother of course, whom he manipulated. She rarely said "no" to him.

Then there was Geri. Geraldine Grace Fitzpatrick, the only daughter of Judge Terrance and Corinne Fitzpatrick. Geri was beautiful, red haired, vivacious, loyal, and fun loving. He had lost a lot of sleep remembering every expression and nuance of her face. Nothing made her sapphire-blue eyes sparkle more than some kind of mischief Avery, Mary Alice, and she were planning.

Bah! Avery! John thought. Avery was the fly in John's ointment! Geri had been in love with Avery since they were five years old. John could still see the look of embarrassment and pleasure on Avery's face the first time Geri kissed him. They were maybe six or seven by then. They had not seen John watching from the cover of bushes near the porch. Avery loved Geri as well. They were a perfect match.

Avery was game for any kind of outing, sporting event, or party, whatever. As long as Geri was there, nothing else really mattered. John had to admit it, Avery would be hard to best when it came to winning the hand of Geri because Avery was also handsome, charming in a sincere way, and he was no coward.

Geraldine Fitzpatrick was the one unobtainable thing in John's life, which also made her more desirable. He had vowed to himself he would win her simply because he desired her. Someday, somehow, she would be his! He could easily devise a plan to discredit Avery and take him out of the picture. Geri then would be more open to a new suitor. Yes, that would work; he would plan very carefully.

There were two other women in John's life, Josephine and Mary Alice Windham. These sisters were as different in personality as they were in looks. Josephine, never Jo or Josie, was a dark haired beauty. She was always impeccably dressed in something that showed a flawless figure. However, she, like her mother, was a perfectionist, and this could be tedious at times. It really did not matter however beautiful she was, there was coldness about her green eyes. She seemed to be always calculating something. John had seen other women like Josephine. They scared him! Though as desirable as any, John had sense enough to run from her kind. This was difficult because Josephine had decided John was right for her, and she used every opportunity to her advantage. She plotted and contrived any occasion to be near him and made sure he understood her intent. If they were alone she could be quite convincing. John did not have many scruples left, and someday he might take up her offer, except for one thing, Mary Alice, her sister.

Mary Alice was naturally pretty, lovely in every way. With pale blond hair and fair features, she was the antithesis of Josephine. Sometimes she wore her long hair pulled back, away from her face. When she wore it like this, a man could see the lovely lines of her neck and shoulders. Her eyes were gray to blue-green, depending on the light. Though she looked refined, even delicate at times, she was no hot-house plant. But more than that, she behaved as a lady, not at all forward and obvious like Josephine.

John took a final look at himself in the beautiful, six foot, hall mirror. The same beveled glass mirror that had been a part of his family for at least four generations. He suddenly had a split second of insight, for it seemed that generations of family were looking back at him through the mirror. He knew someday it would be up to him to protect the wealth. He also knew, "money begets money." How many times had he heard his father say these words?

Though Mary Alice was a prize to be sought in her own right, there was also the Windham fortune, which was sizeable. And, she would always be a credit to him, never an embarrassment. John had come to a decision. He would win the hand of Mary Alice Windham, and some day his hands would be on her share of the fortune. Who knew, maybe in time he would come to love her.

For now, he only had to navigate through three to four hours of a very nice party that was next door at Dr. and Mrs. Windham's. He knew he looked elegant in his evening jacket. All he had to do was duck and dodge the unwelcome advances of Josephine, woo the lovely Mary Alice, and steal any and every moment he could manage with Geri. He would really have to be careful about that. Alice and Geri were best friends. They had been neighbors since birth and were only months apart in age. Each knew the other's life like they knew their own. He must make Alice believe he was in earnest about her. He would be charming to her parents, make them believe in his sincerity as well.

A quick glance at his great-grandfather's pocket watch told him he was just in time to fashionably late.

9. PARTY TIME

It was only a short walk from his grand house to the stately looking gray stone next door. John stopped on the first landing to take it all in. He always liked to savor this moment before a party, to mentally prepare for what was to come. There was always the anticipation of some deal in the works. Too, there would be great beauty and usually some sort of drama. That could prove to be amusing unless he was caught up in the middle of it. John had made it a guiding point in life to avoid that at all cost because it never ended well.

The house had been decorated with flowers from the garden in the side yard. They were the flowers of early summer; peonies, roses, snapdragons and iris. The fragrance gave just a hint of the beauty that was before him. Candles burning in hurricane lamps gave low light, both welcoming and lighting the way of guests. Everything had that late afternoon, early evening glow about it.

Funny, he chose that moment to remember something Mrs. Vivian Windham had told him years ago when he was a child. He had come to their house to play with Alice and Josephine. Mrs. Windham was tending her flower garden, and he had stopped to greet her.

She simply said, "John, did you know that a plant is only as good as its roots?" John did not understand her meaning at the time, he was only a child. He wished he still didn't understand, but he was afraid he was beginning to see the meaning behind the words.

There was a soft summer breeze, a little warmer than usual for that time of year. Dance music was already playing, a familiar, flowing waltz. It was the kind of evening his parents and formal training had taught him to command. His arrival would not be obvious of course, but everyone there would know that John Wallace had arrived.

As he got to the door and knocked, a familiar voice beckoned him. It was Josephine.

"Hello, John. I'm so glad you could come. Please, come in," she said warmly.

She would be perfectly polite in public. It was later that had John worried. "Thank you Josephine. What a lovely evening for the party." He could play this game of cordial pretense too.

As he looked around the room to familiarize himself with who was present, he happened to look up. There, on the stairs, was one of the loveliest girls he had ever seen. Without speaking a word she had the attention of everyone. She was wearing blue silk, just the right shade of blue to enhance the honey color of her skin. It was just a slip of a dress really. There was ruching at the bust line and cap sleeves, the cap sleeves falling slightly off her shoulders. The skirt was gently form fitting and fell gracefully into an ankle length. The only adornment on the dress was a small rhinestone clip at the base of each sleeve. Her hair was pulled away from her face to reveal her grandmother's diamond earrings. Anything more, in John's estimation, would have detracted from her welcoming smile. The look was very soft, feminine—totally approachable.

It was Mary Alice. She was glowing as usual from some inner source. John was going to enjoy this. He smiled back at her, slightly embarrassed, because she had caught him off guard. He had known her all of her life, but never had he seen her looking like this. As he took a step toward her, something else caught his attention. It was laughter from a voice he would know anywhere. It was Geri.

Now this moment was crucial. He must not take his attention from Mary Alice. That would betray his real intent. Could he spare a wasted moment from Geri? He had to! It was the key to the deal. He continued forward to take the hand Mary Alice offered. As he met her, was it possible he saw real interest?

"Good evening, John. I'm so glad you got home in time for my party."

"Thank you for inviting me, Alice. I've never seen you look more beautiful," he replied.

She blushed. He had known she would. She was not as practiced in the art of flirtation as most of the women he knew. She took his offered arm as they went to join the other guests.

Their gracious hosts, Dr. and Mrs. Windham, were welcoming everyone to their home, circulating, making sure everyone was enjoying the party.

As John glanced around the room, he systematically calculated the cost of every dress and the age and value of each piece of jewelry. It was habit. The men he assessed for power. As he did so, his attention was actually caught by Josephine of all the women. He had to admit that at nineteen she filled out her rose colored satin gown nicely! He noticed too, how the color brought a faint blush to her skin and deepened the rose already in her lips. What was wrong with him? What was he thinking? And yet, it was true.

He had caught her in an off guarded moment as Mary Alice had caught him. He also had to admit, at that moment, with the look of vulnerability on her face, Josephine too, was beautiful. These girls had grown up nicely!

Billy Russell came through the front door with some friends from school; all were fashionably dressed in evening attire. He was escorting Frieda Livingston, a pretty, golden haired blond. Her open smile and frilly, yellow dress gave a clue as to her sunny disposition and positive outlook on life. Billy Russell wore a dinner jacket and the youthful anticipation of the evening before him. None of the young adults had serious thoughts or cares this night.

Billy had truly been blessed, for he possessed the gift of charisma in great quantity. He was cool under pressure, but could warm a crowd of people with a firm handshake and genuine smile. The young man was also humble, unassuming. He felt people showed him kindness because of things his mother and father did in service to the community.

He believed men of his own age befriended him because they wanted to get an introduction to his sisters. He had no problem with setting up Josephine, but Mary Alice was entirely different. She deserved someone special.

He weeded out suitors who were not husband material for both, keeping in mind the personalities of the sisters. Mary Alice would have no trouble finding a husband, but Josephine, with her disposition and cool demeanor, that girl would need all the help she could get!

Though Billy looked very grown up, he was still the same sweet spirited, irrepressible youth he had always been. In John's opinion, Billy needed to master the art of restraint.

Billy had no sooner come through the door when Mrs. Windham

asked her son, "Billy, could you and some of your friends take the car, go into town, and pick up some more ice from the ice house? The evening is warmer than I thought it would be, and our other guests will need it as they arrive later."

He eagerly said, "Yes, Ma'am!" to that suggestion. He would grab any excuse to use the car, if only an errand for his mother. Billy told his friends to meet him at the car that was parked behind the house. As they left, Dr. Windham reminded him to, "Take care of the car." There weren't many in a town of this size, and it was a particular amusement for the country doctor who rarely purchased anything unnecessary for himself.

10. A DOG'S LIFE

Billy went through the busy kitchen, then out to the back porch to get a washtub for the block of ice. He also took some old newspapers and a quilt to wrap the ice and keep it from melting.

He stopped long enough to say hello to his hunting dog, Lady, who was waiting for her supper. It seemed everyone had forgotten to feed her because they were getting ready for the party. He went again into the kitchen, found a meaty soup bone, and gave it to her. When he got back to the porch, Bowser, Avery Benton's dog, had followed Avery and Geri from next door. Billy just went back to the kitchen, got another bone, and fed Bowser as well.

Lady was a good hunter, with or without Billy. She could fend for herself if needed, but she was getting older and didn't always feel like hunting. If Billy Russell was going hunting, that was different. She always wanted to go just for his company. He had been her boy for seven years. She had watched him grow from boy to man, almost.

The other dog, Bowser, was different. He was a dog with an attitude and a purpose. Other than the usual, protect master and family, the thing he had dedicated his life to since puppy days was simply this, to make John Wallace's life a living nightmare. He really did not have to try that hard to do it either. John had been sufficiently scared as a boy. Now, all he had to do was lower his head and squeeze his eyes to slits or crouch a little. But his all time favorite thing—and he reserved this because overuse would kill the effect—his favorite intimidation tactic was to sniff at John's ankles, turn his head slightly, and yes, growl, just a little. The dog could barely keep from rolling on the ground in laughter just thinking about the look on John's face. He really should be ashamed, but he wasn't.

It wasn't Bowser's fault. John was always making some remark to Geri, indicating that he would be better for her than Avery. Everybody, including the dog, everybody, except John, rejoiced in the fact that Geri and Avery had found each other. They knew they belonged together, their parents and friends knew it, other suitors knew it. For some reason John just did not get it! He persisted in trying to come between Avery and Geri.

John Pruitt Wallace had another thought coming if he actually believed for half a second that he, Bowser, one of a trio, would allow that to happen!

Bowser went with Avery and Geri everywhere. If they went for a ride in Geri's little blue coupe, Bowser sat in the back seat. How he loved that car! He felt so free, maybe a bit invincible with the air blowing his ears back. Bowser knew one thing for sure—*John would not be breaking up his happy family!*

11. COOL AS MINT

Billy Russell and his friends drove through town to the ice house. It was just a shed built on the side of a dug out hill and was kept locked even though the key always hung in plain sight. He got the key, put the block of ice in the tub, and covered it with the newspapers and the quilt. He would pay for it tomorrow. The small town was big on trust.

On his way out of town, Billy waved to the constable who was making his final rounds of the night. The constable waved back and called, "See you in a little bit." Though he meant to finish early tonight for the party, sometimes his rounds took longer than usual. This had been one of those nights. There had been lots of strangers in town because the train could not go any farther. He knew people genuinely needed help, and he did not want to seem unfriendly. He took time and care with each one until it seemed all had settled for the night.

Henry checked the last store on the last street, everything seemed fine. He would head for home, a small farm just outside of town. The constable had brought a wagon to town to carry supplies back for his livestock. He covered everything with a tarpaulin and called to the horse, "Come up!"

Before he went to the party, he needed to unload the wagon and throw some hay to the horses. He reasoned he could be a little late and everyone would understand. Tardiness, in his case, was in everyone's best interest.

He was right. Everyone welcomed him. He got there just as they sang "Happy Birthday". Billy Russell shook his hand and gave him a large piece of birthday cake. It seemed the retired teacher who became a constable had not only found a new job, but a real home as well.

There were, however, a few strangers he had not seen. They too had made rounds of the town until they found what they were looking for, an unlocked window at the bank.

12. BACK TO THE PARTY

The elegant musical ensemble began the first strains of another song. At about that time, John caught a glimpse of Josephine making her way toward him, so he simply turned to Alice and asked her to dance. She accepted. How elegant they looked together with their opposite physical features. How beautifully they moved, each step matched. To John's surprise, he found conversation with her just as easy.

"John, it will be so good to have you home again. I know your parents have talked of nothing else. By the way, where are your parents?"

"They'll be along shortly," he assured her. "Father was running a little late at the bank, some sort of unexpected deposit came in. Mother was going to wait a bit for him. They wouldn't miss one of your mother's parties. Actually, Mary Alice, many of my most pleasant memories have been evenings here with your family."

"Thank you, John. You're very kind to say so. Have you seen Avery and Geri yet?" she asked.

"Not yet, but I'm looking forward to it." *If she only knew how much,* he thought. The song came to an end, and he escorted her from the dance floor.

The music was drawing to a close as Everett McKenzie came through the Windham's front door. He saw Mary Alice immediately and was mildly aware of someone close to her, a man, but at that moment everything else in the room was a blur of form and color. He saw only her. She had always been pretty, the girl next door, a perfect bud of promise, and now the realization of that promise, the bud opening into flower. Head to toe, inside out, she was everything he had ever wanted in a woman.

John had no more than thanked Mary Alice for the dance, when the firm, tanned hand and beckoning look of another led her away without the slightest glance backward.

It was as though John were a piece of furniture, inconsequential to the whole scene. He felt himself to be a man of some importance and would doubtless become even more so. It was somewhat of a blow to his ego.

So far, this evening had not gone as John had planned. He had never liked Everett; the man was too good, always working, thinking ahead, disgustingly happy.

In truth, Everett reminded John of himself, with a few exceptions of course. Everett was a dreamer, John, a realist. Everett would undoubtedly show mercy if a deal went sour. John would not. This, to John, was the most important factor in the success of a man. He had seen fortunes won and lost because of this one determining human impulse, the ability to survive even if it meant the ruin of another. Everett, he knew, lacked the killer instinct.

The beauty of the girl and the desire to outmaneuver a good man in the deal made Alice a very desirable prize. Winning would be sweet!

From the moment he entered the room, Everett saw only Mary Alice. She had been watching for him. He drew her with his eyes into the embrace of his arms—she was already in his heart. He didn't need to say anything; he just smiled, took one of her hands, and gently led her away from John onto the dance floor. They flowed into the music effortlessly.

There was no need for a lot of small talk, but he knew there must be for the sake of good manners and social graces. Also, no woman wanted to be taken for granted. They had been apart for several months, and all he could think of was how badly he wanted to hold her even closer and share one long, slow kiss.

Should he begin with a compliment? Yes. That would do it. A compliment of beauty was always a good ice breaker, he reasoned. "Alice, you're looking more beautiful than I remember. Do you know you have the attention of every man here?"

She had heard what he said, but his eyes had said so much more. She couldn't tell him all that was in her heart, not yet any way. Instead, she smiled demurely and said, "Thank you, Everett. I *am* very happy tonight. I'm sure that's what you see." All the while she was thinking, *do you know how much I have missed you?*

The dance continued and Everett changed the subject. He asked, "How does it feel to be twenty-one?"

Alice leaned back, took a deep breath, and sighed, "I feel carefree. Whatever happened yesterday is gone, and tomorrow's troubles, whatever they may be, will just have to wait. Tonight is mine! I'm surrounded by people who love me, and at this moment, things could not get much better."

Everett only smiled and said, "Oh, I think they might."

Dr. and Mrs. Windham were working their way through guests, greeting everyone. They were sincere in their joy tonight, very gracious and humble.

John knew this would be a good time to speak to Dr. Windham about Alice. Though they had all grown up together and were good friends, it was the correct thing to do, to formally ask permission to court Alice.

John greeted his hosts, "Dr. Windham, Mrs. Windham, good evening. What a wonderful party!"

"Thank you, John" Mrs. Windham beamed. She loved evenings like this. Any excuse to dress beautifully and decorate the house with flowers from her garden pleased her very much.

As John nodded to his host and hostess, Dr. Windham said, "It's very good to have you here tonight, John. I know you just arrived home yesterday. Have you seen Mary Alice yet? In the time you have been gone, she and Josephine have grown up before our very eyes."

"Indeed, they have," John agreed. "Actually, I wonder if I might have a word with you about Mary Alice."

"Why don't we go into the library for a moment," the doctor led the way.

The library, though small, was quiet and welcoming, adequate for the needs of a country doctor. They sat for a moment. Dr. Windham knew exactly what John wanted, but he actually enjoyed John's moment of uncertainty of the best way to broach the subject. That moment was short lived. It was very clear John had had similar conversations before because of his finesse with words. John opened with how lovely Alice and Josephine had become and his long held, high regard for the family. He closed with the awareness of his own need to find someone with whom to share his life and the assurance that it would end as family or friends.

As he listened, Harrison Windham casually leaned back in his oak and leather chair, looked at the young man, and felt pity for him. John knew the right words to say, but Harrison knew the cost and worth of each word.

He said, "John, you obviously are quite acceptable to my family. Certainly, in the affairs of the heart, no one knows how a thing will develop. You may see Alice, but if it does not work out, do not hurt her by letting her be the last to know or by allowing her to hear it from anyone else. Do we have an agreement?"

"We do!"

As they stood, Harrison offered John his hand to seal the deal. As John took the offered hand, he somehow wondered if there had been a misstep on his side of the bargain. John had been in similar situations, but never this close to his home and family. He had gotten what he wanted, but felt at the same time something else, a little threatened perhaps? There was something about the circumstance that made him feel there was more at risk than he could see at the moment. It was just a feeling, probably.

13. JUGGLING

The party was in full swing when they rejoined the others. Harrison excused himself and resumed his duties as host. John surveyed the room, and to his great delight, he found Geri *alone* at the punch bowl.

A quick glance told him Avery was not near, but where was he? Avery Benton was never very far from Geri.

John quickly thanked his lucky stars and asked Geri to dance. It would have been rude and thoughtless of her to refuse. They had, after all, been childhood friends.

"Hello, John. It's so good to see you." She genuinely welcomed him because it had been a long time since they had seen each other. As they began to dance, Geri continued the conversation, "Now that Everett and you are home, it seems we'll all be together again. It will be like old times, even better. Let's all go to Nashville and have dinner at one of the grand hotels. There's room for six in Daddy's touring car. How about it? Let's do that before everyone gets busy this summer."

John looked into her sparkling eyes and said, "Geri, I have missed you so. You're always so much fun, like the little sister I never had. Yes, we'll do that!" He was proud of himself for not giving away his true feelings. Patience was the order of the night.

What temptation! Here he was—holding her in his arms. He had to resist the desire to hold her closer than convention would allow, and he had just asked for permission to court Geri's best friend. He could only imagine his face in her hair, whispering in her ear. What would she smell like? Better, what would a kiss taste like?

Stop thinking like that, he ordered himself. There would be a time and place for all, but this was not it. He needed to win Geri's trust. His feelings for her had always been too obvious. He knew he should act disinterested for now, and someday, though common knowledge and widely assumed Geri and Avery would wed, John would woo and win Geri. He was sure of it. He might marry Alice, eventually love her, but he was obsessed with Geri.

The dance ended too quickly. John held Geri as close as he dared, her arm anyway, and escorted her from the dance floor. He was about to say something else when Avery slipped his arm around her waist, pulled her close, and kissed her cheek. She giggled, closed her eyes, and reminded him they were in public. Avery laughed. He was in love with the girl and didn't care who knew it.

John pretended to laugh with them as he extended his hand to Avery. Avery pretended he was glad to see John and welcomed him home. The rules of social decorum and good manners needed to be followed tonight. It was a party; they were in someone's home. Avery could momentarily forget the years of innuendo to Geri and the slights to himself. John needed to be taught a lesson and he would oblige, but it could not be tonight, not here.

John had never fooled Avery. They had seen each other grow up and mature. They shared secrets and each knew the nature of the other. A few years away from home might smooth out the rough edges of a personality, but smooth edges would not change a person's nature.

The three continued to exchange cordial bits of news until the music started again. Without asking, Avery took both of Geri's hands, pulled her onto the dance floor and whisked her away to her rightful place, the circle of his arms.

That was John's cue to circulate. He couldn't bear to see the pleasure in Avery's face. He could only remember his own thoughts while dancing with her.

He reminded himself he had work to do and then set out to find Mary Alice. She was dancing with Everett, and there were others just waiting to dance with the "birthday girl." It was her party and she would be obligated to at least speak for a few moments with everyone there.

14. GENTLEMAN FARMER

Though John saw his chance to dance with Alice was at hand, before he could approach, Everett had his arm around her waist and was leading her out to one of the porches. He really would have to deal with Everett, and soon. The gentleman farmer was quickly becoming a nuisance, a complication to his plan.

Instead of asking Mary Alice to dance, Everett had leaned in close and whispered, "Come out to the porch with me."

She smiled her approval and they went out into the soft light of the evening. He couldn't wait to see the expression on her face; it would mean so much to him to give her something. "I've got your birthday present, Mary Alice."

She looked at him not knowing what to say. "Open it," he encouraged.

She carefully pulled away the ribbon and paper and opened the box. Gently, she touched his arm and looked into his eyes, "Everett, it's beautiful," she said softly.

Looks of complete trust and faith were exchanged at that moment. It was as if the years of separation had fallen away, and they were still the same innocents they had been as children.

She knew it really wasn't proper, but she didn't care. Alice kissed his cheek and whispered, "Thank you."

They were too close. They had been in love for a very long time, but admitted it only to themselves. Now they were admitting it to each other.

Everett pulled her closer, kissed her, and said, "Mary Alice, I'm in love with you, and I'm hoping you feel the same way about me."

The necklace was really beautiful, but he had given her so much more. In those few words he had made clear the unspoken. She had always known he loved her, but by saying it, the words resonated as truth. She was sure of it. She also knew that if she had ever thought of loving anyone else, she had been lying to herself.

She clung to him, face to face, knowing if there was such a thing as a perfect moment, this was it. She knew he was waiting for her to say something, but she had waited a long time to hear those words and she wanted to get it right. She looked at him and said, "As long as the rain falls / as surely as a whippoorwill calls / I will always love you too, Everett." She kissed him then, softly, warmly, and passionately.

Everett suddenly realized she had not been asleep all those years before. She had not only heard him, but remembered for nine years every word. They both stood there in the quiet, enjoying the complete bliss of the moment. They loved each other for who they were and that alone.

She moved her hair to one side to allow Everett to fasten the clasp of the necklace. With the choker in place at the base of her throat, she turned to him and asked, "Is it pretty?"

"Beautiful," he said, looking at her and not at the necklace, for she was everything to him. He kissed her again, holding her close for just one more moment, enjoying the sweet fragrance that was Mary Alice. They wanted to stay where they were more than anything, but instead he asked, "Shall we go back inside?"

She smiled and nodded. As they came back into the party, the first person to see them was Harrison. One look at them put his worries to rest. His daughter would be loved greatly! This was a merger in the making even John Wallace could not break, though Harrison was sure John would try.

15. ROSE SATIN

John knew he would have to wait a while to dance again with Mary Alice. It had been a long day and a lovely party with wonderful food and drink—fancy sandwiches, cake, and rosy lemonade made with fresh, sliced strawberries. Why not enjoy a walk in the garden? His hostess had one of the finest ornamental gardens anywhere. He had walked a little farther than planned when he heard something. Someone, a woman, was crying in the darkness. John could not imagine what this was about, so out of curiosity, he went to find her.

There, sitting on a large rock in a rose colored satin gown, was Josephine. She was doubled over, crying into her hands, oblivious to anyone around her.

"Josephine?" John called, disbelieving.

She abruptly stopped crying and blushed in embarrassment.

Again he asked, "Josephine, is that *you*?"

She started crying again. John remembered his handkerchief and his manners. He helped her stand, gave her the handkerchief, and suggested that she, "Breathe slowly."

"Josephine, what is it? Why are you out here crying instead of enjoying the party?"

Josephine had no words for him at that moment. How could she explain her reason for crying? She could not tell him the truth, which was simply that she couldn't think of a tactful way to ask *him* to dance with her. She was tired of being so obvious in her advances toward him. She had embarrassed herself too many times in any number of ways. She wanted John to pursue *her* for a change. She knew she was a beautiful woman. She had been told that often enough by many men. Why did the one man she truly wanted run from her every invitation?

She knew she had to tell John something, so she dried her eyes and said, "It's nothing." She continued, "Things just don't always go the way you think they will."

How well he knew that. She returned his handkerchief, but tears still escaped. John gently touched each one with the folded cloth. Neither of the young adults had ever seen the other like this. He was so sincere in his concern for the crying girl, and she, so vulnerable, not at all forward.

"Jo, rose satin is not meant for rock sitting and tears. Why don't you go thru the back door, go upstairs and fix your face. Meet me on the landing of the staircase in about five minutes. I very much would like to dance with the prettiest girl at the party tonight. Actually, I was looking for you before I came out here."

He had called her "Jo." No one had ever called her by a nickname. She decided she liked it. Maybe the evening wouldn't be a complete failure after all. She nodded in agreement, managed a half smile, and repeated, "Five minutes, okay."

As he watched her go, he couldn't keep from thinking how truly gracefully she moved. The deal broker within him shook his head and scolded, *John, what are you doing?*

John's humanity answered, *Just giving a little hope, that's all. Hope goes a long way you know.*

Yeah, I've heard that before. Just you wait and see. Remember what your mama says, 'This will come home to roost.'

The argument within continued. *I couldn't help it. You saw the look on her face. She needed those words. Now hush for a while. I'm going inside and dance with two of the prettiest girls here. If I can catch the third one without Avery, I'll dance with her too. You can scold me later.*

As he walked to the stairs, she was just coming down. He offered his hand and led her to the center of the floor. This girl, in any dress, especially rose satin, would be lovely swaying to a waltz and John knew just the right moves to show off both.

They made quite a handsome couple. It was John's intent to make Jo feel beautiful, the center of attention, not just the middle child as she had been for seventeen years. Mission accomplished! John was very good at everything he did.

The song came to a close as John deftly turned Josephine in one last, slow spin and came to an artful stop with her and the satin dress draped elegantly in his arms. She held the pose for a moment then straightened, still holding one of his hands. As the party goers applauded their performance, John lifted the hand he held to his lips. Without losing eye contact, he kissed her hand and smiled an engaging smile as he led her to a quiet corner of the room.

Josephine Clarice Windham was not usually at a loss for words, but tonight had proven to be the exception. What does one say about perfection? Besotted, stunned? These words came to mind. Confusion maybe? Who knew tenderness was the key to this man? All of this time she had thought men wanted confidence in a woman. That had worked on some men, up to a point. She would have to rethink her game plan.

John thanked her for the dance and excused himself to talk to other guests. That was okay with Josephine. They had shared something real in the garden, which was so much more than she had hoped. It was certainly more than she could have contrived. The dance had been the "icing on the cake."

16. GUESTS?

The party had been quite a success, an evening to remember in many ways. Dr. and Mrs. Windham said goodnight to each guest and thanked them for coming to celebrate with them.

John had asked to see Mary Alice the following day and speak privately with her about the conversation he had had with her father. She smiled sweetly, agreed, and invited him to have tea, four o'clock in the garden.

Everett wished them goodnight with a gracious smile for Vivian, a firm handshake for Harrison, and a quick kiss on Alice's cheek. He smiled and whispered, "Happy Birthday," to cover his real reason for kissing her in public. He fooled no one. The look in his eyes said everything. He cared deeply for this girl, and she momentarily forgot to breathe. She colored, thanked him again for his gift, and said, "Goodnight."

While the train was still an hour away from town, Mason had awakened from a dream with the voice of his mother screaming to him, *Wake up! Wake up before it's too late!*

Pretending sleep, he overheard Dexter and Farley laughing about robbing and beating a man, a victim from the time before he started running with them. Mason didn't know what he would do next, but one thing was sure, he would go no further with these insanely sick and crazy men.

He had felt the train begin to slow just a bit. Maybe it would be enough. Without a word to them, he stood, went to the open boxcar door, and jumped. The fall was awful. He felt every blow as he hit trees, brush, and rocks all the way down a ravine. If he died, at least he had never killed anyone. It was only a matter of time for Dexter and Farley. Their end was very near, and Mason knew it. He would not be a part of it. If he lived, well, he would figure that out later.

There had been other guests at the party, but these were not received socially. Though there had been lots of food, these guests were not bidden to eat.

Dexter Hughes and Farley Briggs were hungry for more than food as they waited, watching the party from outside the Windham home. They were sick of running and sick of each other, but would endure if it meant getting a lot of money. They had been sitting in front of the open window at the train station and overheard the message about the rail line deposit. They had tried robbing the bank, but the money was not there. That was not going to be a problem; there were other ways to get money.

Now they were sizing up the people of the town, separating rich from poor. It was always good to know whom to threaten, who would pay, who could not. Hiding in the bushes and watching people at a party was probably not the best way to evaluate them, but it was all Dex and Farley had at the moment. Information was always a good thing to have. Details weighed heavily in their line of work, but they had learned to make do with whatever they had.

Even though guests were arriving and leaving most of the evening, the dogs did not stir. Everyone was thankful for that! The constant din of barking dogs would have killed the mood of the party. Dexter and Farley had been very lucky tonight. As far as the dogs were concerned, the men were just two more guests, nothing more.

Lady had been relieved from her hunger and was all too happy to gnaw quietly for the rest of the evening on her soup bone.

Bowser only had one person on his mind. He had almost growled when John was walking in the garden. Almost—until he realized John was with Josephine, and that might not be a bad thing. Bowser had contemplated the situation, *Another occasion then, John.* He would let this one slide; he could be generous.

Petey was quite in his cage now. Mary Alice was in her bed remembering the whole day. It had been the best birthday of her life.

She was pretty sure she knew what John wanted, and she was willing to entertain the idea of courting him, but they would never be more than friends.

Everett already had her heart. She had given it willingly so many years ago. She was not going to give up time with Everett to meet social obligations with John. She needed to be very clear about that. She would, as sincerely possible, explain this to John, thank him for his friendship, and ask him to be happy for them.

She went to sleep then, birthday wishes fulfilled. "Happy Birthday, Mary Alice!"

17. SMALL KINGDOM

Ah, her memories, how the old woman loved them, but now the sun had burned off the morning dew. She had used the excuse of letting her skirt dry from the dew long enough.

She needed to go into the back garden next. The green beans there, were ready too. While they were young and tender, that's when they were best, before they lost their flavor, before the often harsh sun and heat of the day had withered them, before bugs and animals began to tear at them.

Again she donned her sun bonnet, but this time, picked up a larger basket. Perhaps she would find a ripe tomato to go with the beans.

Wading into the beans, she noticed the plants looked good, straight and sturdy. She also noticed some vines creeping into her small kingdom. That would never do. Honeysuckle and morning glory had their place, but it was not among these prizes. Maybe tomorrow she would pull weeds here before the errant vines had a chance to choke her darlings.

She worked through the rows, picking all that was ripe, leaving the smaller produce to mature another day or two. The crop was very good this year.

There was an abundance of mint too. Wild mint was a wonderful plant, but as far as she could tell, its only purpose was to refresh in some way. Mint tea was very good, her favorite, but in addition to that, you only had to softly brush a leaf, and it would release a gentle fragrance. More pressure than that, if a stem was broken or a leaf crushed, the essence of the mint would spread, covering whatever it touched.

She had picked through all of the beans now, and several of the tomatoes were ripe too. It had to be about midday from the position of the sun.

She settled again in her old chair and began rocking, cooling in the shade of the porch. The chair creaked as if reminding her of the past, all it had seen and heard.

She sipped her tea and again started to break the beans. She had more than enough for a "mess." Mess was a word older people in the country used to describe enough of something to cook for a meal. Funny, she thought, the word "mess". How appropriate for the memory that was coming to her now.

18. BANKER'S HOURS

Even though it was Saturday Morning and the bank was closed, Vernon Wallace got up early, dressed quickly, and hurried downstairs to his car. There, on the ground beside the driver's door, was the key he had lost the night before. He could not believe his good fortune! Greatly relieved, he paused for a moment, exhaled a sigh of relief, and silently gave thanks.

Realizing he didn't have to go to work, he went back inside and decided to have breakfast with extra coffee. As he enjoyed the second cup, some unresolved question, a nagging shadow, began to form in his mind. *What if?* He tried to put the feeling aside, but it kept coming, louder each time; he could not quiet the specter. The question quickly turned into—*maybe I'll just go check*.

It was a good thing the bank was not far because the conscientious bank manager grew more anxious as he got closer to the bank. So much so, when he got there, he fairly dove through the front door. Everything looked okay. The roll top on the desk was closed.

He looked toward the safe. It too was closed, but his heart sank. The door was *not* aligned. He knew before he opened it. He looked anyway—he *had* to look. Fifty thousand dollars was gone! With his back to the wall of the safe, he slowly sank to the floor. His confused mind was unable to fully comprehend what his eyes told him to be fact. He sat there in shock, staring at the empty space. In twenty years of banking, he had *never* been robbed. What was he supposed to do now?

When his breathing returned, it came as a gasp. Eventually, he realized he should go tell the constable. Yes, he must start there.

19. HEADS UP, JO

Earlier in the week there had been a great rain storm. Bridges and low lands flooded; train tracks washed out in places. Yesterday, Friday, had been beautiful, morning through about midnight. A light shower came through and the sky had cleared. This morning the horizon was aglow with a red cast, and a few low clouds loomed in the west. Today would be different in *so* many ways.

Everyone at the Windham house went about their usual Saturday routine. About two o'clock in the afternoon, Alice went upstairs to think about what she would tell John at Tea. Josephine decided to get a book and read for a while.

She had been in the library getting a book when she thought she saw John walking in his side of the garden. She decided she would go speak to him. What could she use for an excuse? Jo thought for a moment—she really should thank him for his courtesy last night. He had been her "knight" to the rescue. When she got to the garden, she realized she must have just missed him.

Too bad, she thought.

On the other hand, it would give her more time to think of what to say at their eventual meeting. She had learned last night she must not appear so forward around John. That seemed to repel him. She sighed in frustration—she knew she would have to play the "poor, helpless me; you're so wise card." She could just gag thinking about it. Still, it had worked last night. That had been real. Maybe she should just try not being so obvious. She needed to talk to Mary Alice. Her sister had mastered this skill.

As she leaned against the low, rock wall to enjoy the last, warm rays of sun, Delilah came over. She too had been hunting, butterflies and other small prey. Delilah, like her mistress, was a beauty. The cat was perfect, a Persian mix with long, silky, luxuriant, gray fur and fiery green eyes. She caressed Josephine's feet and ankles with her body and tail. Josephine leaned down to stroke the cat, picked her up in her arms, and hopped up to sit on the low garden wall. Delilah squirmed, preferring to sit on the ledge beside her and enjoy the sun.

Josephine closed her eyes to relish the warmth, totally relaxed. She never saw or felt, until it was too late, the hands around her mouth and waist. She was forcefully pulled backward over the wall until she was on the ground. She fought against them, kicking and screaming, until someone quickly blindfolded and gagged her. Next, she could feel her hands and feet being tied. Then she was off the ground.

Josephine was too stunned to think. She was disoriented completely. *What had happened?* Terrible confusion set in, then disbelief that something like this could be happening. *No! She refused to think that!* Tears filled her eyes. *How many times had her parents warned her and her siblings about strangers? But she had not seen anyone. No, wait. She had seen a man she thought was John.* Then she knew what she dared not think. *She was being kidnapped!*

She felt her arms being scratched by bushes as she was carried through what must have been the back yards of neighbors. Then she felt her body being hoisted up and slung over the back of one of the men like a sack of potatoes.

They took turns carrying her like this for several minutes. She reasoned they were in the woods because what little light she had grew darker. She could hear rushing water and smell the vegetation, the sweet clear smell of mint crushing under their feet.

She was thrown into something, *a boat perhaps?* She heard the paddles hit water and had the sensation of moving, floating. Again she was picked up, carried, and finally landed on solid ground. One of the men spoke.

"What are we gonna' do now?" asked an anxious voice.

"We wait," answered the voice of the one who had done this before.

20. BANKER BLUES

Constable Henry Milton returned with Wallace, looked at everything, and said, "Yep, you been robbed." All he could add was that everything was locked up tight when he made his rounds for the night.

Though the reality of the situation was clear, Vernon Wallace was in shock and found the situation impossible to believe. Suddenly, nothing was making any sense. He rehearsed the events again and again in his poor, trapped mind. It always came out the same. He ran for the men's room; he was going to be sick!

Henry Milton had seen this before. He knew his friend needed to go home and rest if possible. There was nothing else that could be done at the bank.

He drove Wallace home and helped explain to the banker's family what had happened.

Then, thinking a house call might be in order, Henry went next door to get Dr. Windham. The doctor immediately recognized the classic symptoms of shock and gave Wallace something to make him sleep. A few hours of escape could refresh an exhausted mind and give family and friends a chance to think.

John could not believe this himself. He ran to the car and drove to the bank as quickly as possible, as though that would change anything. He might as well be closing the gate after the cows were out.

He found the bank just as his father and the constable had said. As far as he could see, only the railroad deposit had been taken. As John thought it through, he realized it was probably easier to grab a filled satchel and run, than take the time to gather any more money from still further enclosed containers within the vault. Whoever took the money evidently thought "in and out quickly" made more sense than taking a lot of time with the robbery. There was less chance of being caught anyway.

21. NEVER ASK

John drove home from the bank more than a bit stunned. Poor John, little did he know his world was about to be "rocked" further.

As John opened the front door of his home, he noticed a folded piece of paper. It read:

WE'VE GOT YOUR GIRLFRIEND. IF YOU WANT TO SEE HER ALIVE, BRING $50,000 TO THE COVERED BRIDGE SUNDAY NIGHT. WAIT UNTIL DARK, COME ALONE. WE'LL BE WATCHING!

"What is this?" John wondered aloud. He read it again, three times to be exact. *Could this all be a really bad joke? Oh, please let it be. What is happening?* Suddenly, nothing in John's life was making any sense. The bank robbery had already been the worst shock of his life, but this, this was just too much.

He sat there in the open front doorway because he could do no more. Suddenly, a thought struck him. *Who had been kidnapped?* He did not have a girlfriend. His mind raced ahead, lurching at times as he realized the only girls he knew were Mary Alice, Josephine, and Geri.

"Oh, No!" he begged, "Please not Geri." And if not Geri, who then?

John had danced with all three of the girls at the party, but he had talked in the garden with Josephine. He had even dried her tears.

"Oh, dear Lord," he prayed, his mind fast forwarding. How was he going to break this news to Harrison and Vivian?

He would not go into his house to check on his father. That would have to wait. If what he thought was true, someone's life was about to be shattered. John prayed he was wrong on this, but his gut feeling told him he was not. All three of these girls were dear to him. *Why had it taken so much time to see this?*

He walked slowly to the house of his friends. He was in no hurry to deliver this news. He desperately needed time to think of a kind way to tell them something that he knew would be devastating to them.

John did not bother to knock. He opened the door carefully and stood very still for just a moment, looking first at Harrison, then Vivian, then back to Harrison.

Vivian was sitting on the couch, sewing in hand. She looked up and smiled gently as if in sympathy for John and his father.

Harrison stood, put down his reading glasses and the newspaper, and asked, "John, is it your father? Has something happened? Am I needed?"

John could not speak at first. Then he slowly began to nod and said, "Yes, I'm afraid something has happened."

Mary Alice came down the stairs at that moment. A grimace of relief flooded over John. The kidnappers did not have Mary Alice. He silently thanked God. Her trusting smile would only defend her belief that all was well for perhaps another moment or two. She could never guess in a million years what was coming next.

Mary Alice, still smiling, called out to him, "John, is it four o'clock already? Do come in. I'll get the things for our tea."

"Mary Alice," John began, "You—all of you need to sit down. I have to tell you something."

Anxiety was rising in the room, almost palpable in the parents. John's face held no hope as he began.

"This is a note demanding money for the return of my girlfriend. Mary Alice is here; where is Josephine?"

Still unmoved by his announcement, Mary Alice replied, "I'll go upstairs and get her."

Everyone held their breath as she checked bedrooms and baths calling, "Josephine? Jo? Where are you?"

She came back to the top of the stairs. The smile was gone. In its place, a furrowed brow and acceptance that what John suggested might be true.

"I can't find her," she began. Why would anyone kidnap Josephine?"

Billy Russell came through the kitchen door then, Lady following close on his heels. "Yes, please tell us why anyone in their right mind would want to kidnap Jo" . . . he stopped short with his question. The look on each face told him he had missed something important.

It was a race to see who cast him the first disapproving look. His family seemed horrified with the question. He quickly recanted his words.

"Sorry, sorry, it was just a leftover from childhood."

Actually, there was a time when anyone in that room would have asked the same thing. They were all grown now, and this was not a childhood game.

He continued, "Are you serious? She was just outside—reading in the garden."

Everyone turned and ran outside, hoping against false hope to find her there. She was not. Only her book remained as it had fallen. Delilah was still asleep on the half wall, untouched, her muscles briefly twitching in response to some butterfly chase sequence in a dream.

Vivian tried to put on a brave face, but a low moan escaped that quickly turned into sobs and wails. Harrison walked with his arm around her for support, leading her back inside the house. All he could understand from Vivian was, "I cannot lose another child. I can't go through that again." Her eyes begged him to take back the words that led them to this moment. He could not.

He tried to soothe her with comforting words but fooled no one. Though Harrison was dealing with a resurgence of his own grief, he needed to be strong for both of them. For now, he knew he needed to think clearly. Anguish over the past and apprehension from what might be would have to wait. He could not afford to give in to those emotions yet. Maybe he could be strong, for a little while at least. Josephine needed her father like never before. He would not fail her because of a weak, fearful moment.

Vivian needed to NOT think. In her present state she was 'borrowing trouble' according to her Aunt Lucy, and that might not be necessary. Harrison went to his bag again for something to alleviate the pain of anguish.

He managed to get Vivian settled upstairs in their bed and came back down.

"John," he asked, "could I see the note?" They reread it.

"The railroad money is gone," John reminded.

"I know," Harrison replied, "I'll just have to get what money I can together and pray it is enough."

He went to the library and closed the door. The safe under the bookcase in his office was hidden. He had always known there was a great deal of money there, but chose not to think about it.

His father-in-law, Thomas Morton, had shown him the safe and the money years ago. He made Harrison and Vivian promise never to tell anyone else. They had kept that promise.

Both of Vivian's parents came from "old money". The cash was only for an emergency. There was more—much more—in banks, stocks, and trading companies around the world. Harrison cared nothing for the money. His only thought was for Josephine and her safe return. He had seen money open doors of opportunity, and it could accomplish incredibly good things. In this case, it seemed to have made them a target.

Harrison counted what he needed, came back to the living room, and told John he should make the delivery since the note had been sent to him. Harrison would be close in case he was needed.

It had already been a long day, and John realized he needed to check on his father. The middle aged man was scared. The robbery was the worst thing that had ever happened in his life. He needed to know John and the constable were working to find the money. John decided not to tell Wallace Sr. about the ransom note, not until he absolutely had to anyway.

22. LITTLE BROTHER

Earlier, while Harrison was taking Vivian upstairs to rest, Mary Alice and Billy Russell went outside to talk. Billy dragged Alice down to the grove of trees, the place where they had gone for years to plot away from the ears of safety conscious parents. He knew they could not afford to be overheard on this one.

"Alice, I'm not going to stand around and wait while someone threatens our family and hurts our sister. We could go out tonight and search some very good hiding places where they might have taken her. There's the bridge, the old barns behind the Miller place, and the island. We could have her home and safe by morning," he reasoned.

She already knew where this was going, shook her head, and gave him a firm, "No! We could mess up negotiations for her too!"

He continued, "Well, if you won't help me, then I'll just go alone."

Alice had heard this before. He was always running ahead on impulse rather than reason. "Billy, please don't do this. I know you want to help, but this will not. It could make things a lot worse."

"Okay. Maybe we won't try to rescue her, but we need to look for her. If we could find her, that would be good, wouldn't it? It would give us an edge if something goes wrong."

He had done it again. He had found a hole in her argument of logic and common sense. She had to agree, knowing Jo's location would be an advantage if it came to confrontation with these men. She knew their father would do all he could to assure a happy ending, but sometimes information could be a deciding factor, especially if things did not go as planned.

"All right," she said, knowing in her heart she would regret it, "but after Mom and Dad get settled for the evening."

Neither Alice nor Billy could know this yet. Parents may get settled, even go to bed, but as long as a child is out, they do not sleep. Their hearts are ever vigilant, searching for signs that all is as it should be. Children are in their places, every breath measured.

Mary Alice did know her little brother would be better off if she went with him. She would at least try to rein him in and curb his impulsiveness. She shook her head, quietly acknowledging to herself, for that would be almost impossible.

Billy went back to the house to pack the gear he thought they would need. He would take his hunting knife. It served as a multipurpose tool. He reached for his gun, hesitated, for he knew if he took it he might have to use it, and picked it up anyway. If this wasn't a time for a weapon, then he couldn't imagine there would ever be a need for one. He would grab the lantern too. He did not know how late it would be when they got home, and it would probably get dark early. Clouds were already rolling in from the southwest. Maybe the clouds would clear. He knew he would go searching for Jo whatever the weather.

23. BREAKDOWN

Mary Alice needed time to think. Everything had happened too quickly. There had been no time to process information, to quiet the tumult going on in her head.

She felt the weight of being the responsible one, and it was all too much. She knew what they were planning was probably the wrong thing to do, but what else could she do? In a way, Billy was right. Jo needed help, and the sooner, the better. What if paying the ransom did not work? What could they do then? At this moment her emotions were screaming, but her common sense said nothing.

This was not like the childish pranks Billy had begged her to be party to in the past. This was real; their lives could be at stake.

"Dear God," she prayed. "What should I do?"

After Billy left, she sat down on the grass under the shade of the trees in the grove. Immediately the hand of a friend reached out, taking her hands into his—it was Everett. He sat beside her and wrapped an arm around her shoulders, pulling her closer to his side. His being there, holding her, started the tears. All she could manage to say was, "Oh, Everett," more tears.

"Shh, it's going to be alright." He cradled her like a small child and kissed her head. "Your dad told me everything. I have to admit it looks really bad, but I'm here and I'll do whatever I can to get all of you through this."

That was exactly what she knew Everett would say. She already depended on him so much.

"What *can* we do?" she asked. "Is there anything we can do to get her back safely?"

"All we can do for now is whatever they tell us to do. They have the advantage. We have few options. You could refuse to pay the ransom, but that wouldn't be wise." He went on. "We have to believe she will be returned. As long as the kidnappers don't feel trapped in a situation with no way out, or pushed into doing something stupid or vindictive, there is no reason NOT to let her go."

"What if she can identify them?"

"If they're smart, they've kept her blindfolded. She won't know what they look like or how many there are either."

"Have you told Geri?" he asked, trying to change the subject.

"No, I was on my way to do that before I sat down."

He pulled her to her feet saying, "Then we'll go together."

24. BEST FRIENDS

They went through the east side of the picket fence around Judge Fitzpatrick's house, to the wide porch on the front of the house. Geri was swinging in the porch swing, and her mother sat in her white wicker rocker. Both were enjoying a Saturday afternoon with a glass of iced tea.

"Afternoon, Miss Corinne, Geri. Fine day for porch sittin,'" Everett greeted them.

"Yes it is, Everett. You all come on up and join us. I'll get you both some tea," Corinne offered in a gracious, easy going voice.

Everett removed his hat as he and Alice stepped up the steps and settled in the wicker loveseat.

Corinne Fitzpatrick was a kind woman and very wise. Though her young friends were cordial enough, she could see from the expression on each face, something was amiss.

When she returned she had other guests. Avery Benton and Bowser had come over to see Geri. He had just finished the day working for his parents at their hardware store, a general store that carried small farming implements, household merchandise and groceries for the town, and offered ice from the ice house. It had been a busy day.

Corinne welcomed Avery and went back to the kitchen for more tea. When she returned this time, there were four somber faces instead of two.

She looked at them, shook her head and said, "No one leaves this porch until somebody tells me what's going on!" She sat down.

"Mom," Geri said, "something awful has happened. Josephine has been kidnapped."

"Oh, Vivian," Corinne cried, "I must go to her at once." She could still remember the agony her friends had gone through with the loss of Sam Jr.

Hurriedly, she left the two worried couples sitting on the porch.

"All right, what are we going to do? We can't just sit here and not act!" Geri was always ready for action.

Avery gave her a warning look and winked so only she saw it. "Geri, this needs to be handled by the family," he said. Looking at Alice he offered, "Mary Alice, we're here if you need us."

Alice thanked them both for their concern and left with Everett. It was going to be a very long night. She keenly felt the burden of safety for her brother and sister. Everett, however, did not need to be in danger. She would not tell him of Billy's plans.

Geri didn't speak at first. She cautioned Avery with a look as she put one finger over her own lips for silence and one finger in the air, warning him to wait. She let her guests get to the back of the house before speaking.

Turning to him she asked, "Well, What are we going to do?"

Cautiously, he began. "We're probably gonna' go find Josie. We're going to look for her anyway. When we find her, if possible, we're gonna' bring her home. I didn't want to say anything in front of Mary Alice and Everett because I didn't want them to worry about us or try to stop us."

There was this impossible grace about the man, always "cool" under pressure. His actions and reactions were almost always correct, and he was lead by right intentions. He just seemed to let things happen as they would, and then he dealt with whatever came next.

He continued, "I would rather go by myself, but I know that won't stop *you*. I fear for you—most of the time actually." He gave a disparaging look, "You and I are so much alike. If we go together, at least I'll know where you are and what you're doing."

Geri had to agree on every point. They were alike in many ways, but she was far more impulsive. She hurried things. She had to admit there had been times in life when she had been downright foolhardy by rushing ahead. She had tried to temper this, but it always seemed to her, other people would just drag along when a matter could be settled, ended. Why wait? With Avery, there had been times when he seemed to move too slowly, but things usually worked out well. In this instance, the safety of their friend outweighed speed. She would just be content to go looking for Josephine for now. If she needed to act quickly later, then she was ready.

Mary Alice could not know Geri and Avery would search that night for Josephine. She would not ask anyone to attempt what she considered a "suicide mission." She and Billy Russell were compelled by familial duty and honor bound to look for their sister.

Though she seriously doubted Billy considered the risk involved, the cost if their plan backfired in some way, she knew Josephine was counting on them. She sighed, it would be easier to know what Billy was doing than *not* to know and worry about him. Her mind settled then, she would go.

25. SEARCH

The rain started about three o'clock in the afternoon. It was nothing major at first; the deluge came later. By six o'clock, dark, ominous, rolling clouds appeared, hanging low, threatening a downpour.

Unsettling wind began stirring the clouds creating an unnerving threat to anyone daft enough to venture out for whatever reason. The storm was just getting started in *so* many ways.

Then lightening arrived, splintering off into every direction, bringing with it a building static that seemed to make the hair on Mary Alice's arms stand erect. But more than that, there was inner turmoil. Her anxiety was growing in intensity. Her mind kept repeating—*this is not right!* She begged the voice to shut up!

Alice and Billy knew they would have only one night to find their sister. They slipped out of the house on some pretense of errands. Harrison, distracted with worry, hardly knew what they said. Vivian was upstairs in the bliss of not knowing anything.

They started with the barns and smokehouses in the area but found nothing. Next, they went over the wooden bridge, just glancing under it. Seeing nothing, they moved on, pretending to be en route south of the town in case the kidnappers were watching.

It was good that they had driven their father's car because the rain was unrelenting. Every time they stopped to check a building, they got even wetter. There was only one more place to look, the overgrown island in the middle of the lake on the Benton's property.

There were huge rocks on the north side with crags jutting outward, a mass of trees and brush in the middle, and some open spaces where people sometimes picnicked.

The dread both felt was growing, quickly turning into fear. This was the last place to search, and the possibility of finding trouble was very real. The chance of finding Josephine was real too. They knew they had to search the small island.

They left the car on the side of the road and walked through the soggy field to the lake. The light of late afternoon was still with them, but it was fading fast because of the low clouds. There was also light from the lightening that sporadically struck all around them. The whole sky it seemed, fracturing, terrifyingly beautiful. Though they carried a lantern, they did not light it. A lantern could alert the kidnappers, and this needed to be a covert mission—quickly in, then out.

The ground in the field was soft, saturated. At times they sank in water up to their ankles. It didn't matter, they were already soaked to the skin, and the rain kept falling.

Undaunted by any of this, they went on. By the time they reached the lake, the little boat that was usually there was barely aground, already half in and half out of the water. Billy shouted, "Get in!" He hurried to get in the boat, pushing the little craft from the shore with a paddle. Alice could already see this was not going well, but they had gone too far to stop now. She could feel herself bracing for whatever would happen next, but she knew better than to ask. They really had not had time to make a plan. It was one of those situations when you hoped and prayed for the best after jumping into it. She grabbed an oar to help Billy, shook her head in a momentary loss of courage, and began to row.

Back at the Benton home, Avery did have a plan and a gun. His party would need both. He got a canoe from the barn and put in from the banks of the creek just out of sight from his house.

The constant rain and thunder did not matter, and there was no room for doubt or fear. With singleness of mind, they would not rest until they had exhausted every possibility of finding Jo.

Earlier, Geri had changed into a shirt and an old pair of Avery's jeans. She got away with the ensemble by calling them her "gardening" pants and saved them for escapades such as this. She told her mother she was going to Avery's for the evening. Corinne had learned long ago there was no point in questioning Geri. She also knew both Geri and Avery were trustworthy, and that was enough. They had grown up together, so informal visits like this were pretty common.

The Judge and Corinne had been invited to supper by some friends in the nearby Chapel Hill area. They couldn't know they would have to stay with these friends until early Monday morning. Several roads would wash out in places during the evening storm.

Avery's parents had plans for the evening as well. They were going almost to Lewisburg, to look at a warehouse closer to Caney. If they could get goods shipped closer to their store, the convenience would be very helpful.

Matthew and Elizabeth Benton would not be able to get home until Monday either because flooding happens in the strangest places. Neither set of parents knew of Avery's or Geri's plans. All believed they would beat the storm.

The current of the creek was swift as Geri and Avery slipped the boat into the water. The stream, already swollen from recent flooding, fed into the lake where the water immediately got deeper. They would have to paddle strenuously against the current to control the direction of the little craft. Bowser stood in the bow of the boat, ever alert and ready for action.

They saw nothing at first, but then the huge rocks of the island came into view. They would come in from the north side, look among the rocks, and then come aground on the east side.

As they came closer, they could see a lean-to had been hastily thrown together. It was nothing more than some rotten planks and brush wood piled over the rocks. It would afford no real protection from the slightest wind, not to mention the monsoon that now drenched them.

Geri yelled over the storm, "Maybe she's there," and pointed to the lean-to.

Avery nodded his assent, while Bowser looked where Geri pointed. They couldn't be sure until they got closer. They pulled around to the side of the island where rocks became dirt and grass. A few young trees gave Avery something to grab. He slowed the canoe while Geri pulled them closer with an oar.

Bowser was the first to jump out of the boat. He instantly began to survey his surroundings with his nose and got a whiff of something. Unsure of what it was, he held his vigilance, cautiously using all of his senses.

Thinking Avery was close behind her, Geri hurried from the bank of the stream. "Wait," he yelled over the noise of rushing water and the storm.

Not hearing Avery's caution to wait and anxious to get a better look, she scrambled up the bank and began climbing onto the slippery, wet rocks.

Avery had his hands full trying to secure the boat in the rushing water and storm. The small trees and bushes near him were big enough, but much of the dirt had washed away exposing slick roots. Without a solid footing, he kept sliding back into the lake, the rushing water swirling around his ankles, washing his feet out from under him.

After many attempts to reach a sturdy branch, he finally succeeded and tied the boat as securely as he could. *Maybe it would hold.* He could see the current was still pulling the back of the canoe. This would *not* do. He took a minute or two more to drag the whole thing out of the water. If he didn't, he knew they could be stranded on the island for a long time.

He grabbed his rifle from the boat and spoke to the dog, "You watch, Boy!" Bowser understood. He knew the command was serious. They were in trouble from the elements if nothing else. Sometimes he questioned the wisdom of humans, but still, he trusted Avery. It must be important or they would not be out on a night like this.

On the other side of the lake, Billy Russell began rowing for the island. The whole night began to feel like a "fool's errand" to Mary Alice. It was now raining so hard their boat was taking on water. It was pouring from their heads, off their clothes, and into their shoes. *Oh well*, she thought, *they could swim for it if they had to.* Jo needed them desperately. They would go on.

It usually took no more than five or six minutes of hard rowing to reach the west bank of the island. Tonight they were facing severe weather, and the rowing took a lot more effort and time.

They knew they were going to have to go through some dense brush and weeds when they got to the island. They had gone there often and knew the terrain well.

Billy steered the boat so it came to land sideways near a thicket. Mary Alice's clothes were so water-logged she could hardly move. Ever eager to move on, Billy hurriedly wandered into the clearing already interested in something, while Alice pulled the boat onto the shore and hid it in the thick reeds. She didn't know why really, it just seemed to make sense. *She must remember to grab the lantern,* she thought. They had needed it already in some places but couldn't chance lighting it. Hastily, she checked on her brother's location.

By now he had put more ground between them and was almost to the other side of the shallow clearing. She could hardly see him. She tromped back into the reeds to get the lantern and turned back around.

Between her and her brother, illuminated by a flash of lightening, there stood the silhouette of a man with a gun aimed directly at Billy. He had appeared out of nowhere.

Mary Alice blamed herself for their present mess. She was the oldest. She knew better than to listen to him, but her little brother had whined and begged until she finally agreed. Here they were *again*. She had told Billy Russell there were situations in life that you might escape only once. They had already cheated fate more than they should have dared. He had not learned anything. And, here she was, trying to save him from certain death at the hands of someone they were yet to meet.

She knew she should not breathe. The sound would give the enemy her location, exactly three feet squarely behind him—so very close. In the fast approaching cover of night, even with the storm crashing around them, he would surely hear her. She was in agony. She needed to scream, to somehow warn her brother of what was imminent. Where had the plan gone wrong? How had they gotten to this point?

She instantly made a mental note for the next time he started begging her. Who was she kidding? There would be no next time. They were not getting out of this one!

On the north end of the island, Geri and Avery had their own problems. By the time Avery got to the rocks, Geri had climbed even farther. She was clawing her way over the largest rock when she slipped.

As she slid she managed to grab part of a thick sheet of rock. There was only room to clutch the jagged sheet with her hands, nothing bigger to grasp, and nowhere to gain a foothold. The expanse below her feet revealed a very long drop onto more jagged rocks.

"Avery!" she screamed, "I can't hold on, hurry!"

"I'm coming," he yelled.

Laying the rifle down, he started the climb.

Bowser suddenly understood why his hackles were standing, why all of his senses prickled on full alert. A sudden strike of lightening flared, causing just a glint of light to be reflected from a pistol barrel. The dog squinted with his eyes until they were slits to get a closer look. Then he saw a man hiding in the dark, jungle like brush, cautiously easing forward, a gun aimed at Avery. Bowser growled a warning to Avery and lunged at the man.

Farley Briggs had no qualms about killing anything. He shot the dog. Bowser fell to the ground with a "yelp."

Hearing this, Avery turned, completely surprised. Farley shot again. This time Avery fell. Briggs cared nothing for either life. His only thought was to get away from the scene. This deal had taken a wrong turn somewhere. There would be no ransom, and if he didn't act quickly, there would be witnesses.

He hurried out of the bushes, pausing to make sure both hits were good. They were. He only needed to do one more thing. He needed to get to the girl hanging from the rock, and he needed to be quick about it.

They had been discovered. How many others were already on the island? His partner, Dexter Hughes, was keeping watch on the south end of the island. He would hear the shots and know something had gone wrong. In that case, they were to get rid of any witnesses and get away from the kidnapped girl as fast as they could.

He climbed out to the ledge where Geri was barely hanging. She thought he had come to pull her up. Her eyes were full of hope and pleading.

"Please," she cried. "Help me!"

There would be no mercy from this man. He pried her hands from the ledge and let go. Her scream lasted only seconds. The last thing she saw was the look of absolute power on the man's face.

Farley jumped from the rocks, grabbed Avery's rifle, and started running for the small waiting boat at the south end of the island.

Upon hearing the two shots from the pistol, Mary Alice, Billy, and the unknown man immediately dropped to the ground and stayed low, shooting crisis averted for the moment. Alice held her breath, silently looking around for whatever would happen next.

Dexter was the first to move. He slipped into the cover of the closest brush; the shots were his cue to abort the plan. This was a first for them. They had successfully pulled it off in other towns. The people were usually just happy to get their family back, and they did not offer resistance. Farley and Dex would regroup and rethink the situation at the dense tree line across the lake.

Staying low to the ground, Dexter inched further into the brush. Believing he had cover then, he stood and began running in earnest to the south bank and the waiting boat.

The din of the storm let up a little, just enough for Mary Alice to hear something else. From the north side, her left, came a thrashing of weeds and brush. Someone else was running, directly it seemed, toward her spot.

Farley kept as much as possible to the partial path. He held Avery's rifle high as he raced for the boat, jumping over low limbs as though they were hurdles in a race.

He was in such a hurry that he did not see Alice as he passed, for she was crouching low in her hiding spot only inches away. She waited until the sound of running faded, and then quickly moved to the last place she had seen Billy. He was still there, safe. As they stared south into the dim light, they could hear the slap of oars hitting water. Their pursuers were leaving, fleeing before they could be discovered.

Alice and Billy had seen two figures; they needed to learn more. Josephine was still missing, and they had heard two shots. Neither of them wanted to speak the words that would bring those two thoughts together.

Clouds were beginning to part and the light of early evening had not faded entirely. Alice began by asking, "Do you think there is anybody else here?"

"We have to check out the north side. I'll be more careful," he promised. The reality of the situation was beginning to dawn on him.

They hurried along the east bank of the island. First, they saw Avery's boat still tied to a tree limb. Finding no one on the bank, they started for the rocks. The two young adults had never been through the emotions that now enveloped them: confusion, disbelief, and horror.

A cry of "No!" escaped Alice

Billy rushed to Avery, and then he saw the dog. Though wounded, the trusted friend had crawled to Avery's side.

"They're both still alive," he said. Immediately he pulled off his shirt, ripping and tearing it to make bandages. While he was packing Avery's wound, he threw his pocket knife to Alice and ordered her to do the same with her skirt. "We'll need more bandages to slow the bleeding."

Incredulously, Alice asked, "What were they doing here?" Of course, she knew the answer to that question. She went on, "Do you think Geri was with them?" Again, she already knew.

"Absolutely!" he answered as he continued to work on Avery. "I'll go look for her, if you'll keep packing these wounds."

He climbed over the rocks to look around. Below him at the water's edge, he could see Geri's twisted and unmoving body. To his left, he saw Josephine.

"I've found her! I've found Josephine," he cried.

Mary Alice did not stop wrapping wounds, but instantly offered, "Thank you, Lord."

Billy climbed over the ledge and boulders to the lean-to. Josephine was blindfolded, but she recognized her little brother's voice. Great tears of relief and thanks washed down her face as he untied her hands and feet.

"Jo, are you alright? Did they hurt you?"

"No, I'm okay. I still cannot believe anyone could be so cruel! They just grabbed me and ran. I was so scared!" she sobbed.

Billy hugged her and quieted her saying, "It's over, Jo. They're gone. I saw them leave. Let's go home."

Jo carefully made her way off the rocks. A heartfelt cry of grief and more tears came as she passed Geri's body.

"I heard Geri call for Avery's help," Jo began. "She was trying to get to me when she fell. Later, I heard a scream—then nothing else."

"I never realized Geri or Avery would go this far to help me," she continued.

They could see Geri on the rocks below. There was no movement except for her beautiful red hair, now flowing gently in the small, lapping waves of the rising water.

"I'll go down and see if I can help her," Billy suggested as he began his descent. He carefully climbed down through boulders and gaps to the girl's still and silent body.

"Geri," he asked, "can you hear me? How badly are you hurt?" She did not move.

Slowly she spoke, "My arm, my head," she moaned, "my side."

He cautioned her to be still. Geri had been knocked unconscious by the fall. Gradually, she was becoming more aware of her surroundings. With consciousness came the awareness of exquisite physical pain. She had broken an arm for sure. He could see that from the angle of the bone. There was also a very good possibility she had a concussion.

Though Billy knew she was hurt, he was quite relieved to hear her speak. Seeing her like that, so still, she had really looked dead. He had never been more afraid in his life than at that moment.

"I've got to get some help to get you out of here. I have to leave you, but I promise to come back." He was about to leave when she asked the question Billy was dreading.

"I know you'll come back. But tell me, where's Avery? Is he alright?"

He thought half a second and answered, "He's—with Mary Alice and Jo. I've got to get you some help." He left quickly before she could ask more.

Though Geri was in a great deal of pain, there was something that troubled her even more. She had heard two shots and Avery had not come to help her. She needed to get to him, to see for herself that he was all right. Billy had not answered her question, he had only evaded it. She tried to get up. The pain on her whole left side, the arm, the ribs—it was too much. *Maybe she could just . . . . The water feels so cool*, she thought, as she passed out again.

When Billy climbed out of the rocks, Alice and Jo were talking to Avery, trying to rouse him. He would be in great pain when that happened. Maybe it was a blessing to not know everything at the present.

His friends didn't know how much Avery could hear. He barely spoke because the effort to breathe was great. It was all he could do to hold on, drifting in and out of consciousness.

Alice took charge. She knew a decision had to be made. Having always been the oldest, this came naturally. By pecking order, Jo and Billy fell in line.

She spoke, "Billy, you take Jo and go for help. I'll stay with Avery and Geri. You're faster, and if you run into trouble you both have a better chance than if I take her home."

For once in his life he did not argue. Josephine had been through enough. She needed her mother as much, almost, as her mother needed her.

Billy would stop first at Everett's farm because it was the closest. He could send Everett back to help Mary Alice before getting his father and some medical supplies. John would be needed too. Billy had a plan and he liked it!

26. SECOND GUESSING

From the tree line Dex and Farley saw two figures cross the marshy field. They had lost their "bait." She was free.

"Are you sure they're both dead?" growled Dexter.

"Pretty sure, there was enough blood on the boy. And the girl, if the fall didn't kill her, then the rising water over the rocks will soon enough," Farley replied. He obviously did not foresee the coming response from Dexter.

"Idiot!" he screamed. "Go back over there and make sure. We don't leave witnesses, ever!"

Though cruel and cautious, Farley was not meticulous with details. He was, in fact, sloppy when completing a task. And, there was the cardinal rule of warfare, never go back. Returning through an enemy line usually proved to be more dangerous than going through it the first time.

"You can go if you feel the need," Farley replied, "I'm not!"

Dex knew Farley was right about going back. He had seen others get caught by returning to a situation once clear.

"This is different. If they're not dead, they can place you with the kidnapped girl. They saw your face. I ought to just shoot you," Dexter suggested. "That would be simpler than trying to clean up your messes."

From the look on his face, Farley wondered if Dex was really considering this possibility.

Dex continued to stare at Farley as if deciding. Farley backed down. Shrugging as though the task before him was needless, he stomped off in the direction of the lake.

This time he walked up the east side, cautiously watching for anyone else who might be there. Seeing no one, he continued. He was almost to the rocks when he heard the voice of a girl. It was Mary Alice, trying to awaken Avery.

Farley looked to see if Alice was alone and then stepped out of hiding. "Don't move," he ordered. Mary Alice saw the gun.

"Is he dead?" Farley asked.

Alice didn't have to guess. She knew from his demeanor, this man was a killer.

"I think so," her reply cautious.

Farley kicked Avery's boot as if to spur some life from his body. Avery did not move. There was a lot of blood, so Farley moved on.

He looked over the rock ledge. Geri did not move. The pool of water around her still body was rising.

Farley was satisfied the witnesses would not be talking. He suddenly had an idea. They had lost the first hostage, but Mary Alice would do just as well for the ransom.

"You're coming with me," he snarled, grabbing her arm. She fought back, kicking and scratching, beating him, trying to push him away, until he slapped her full force with the meat of his hand. Her struggling, weighed against his brutal force, was useless. He coarsely grabbed and held her by the neck of her shirt and growled, "You *are* coming with me!" Again he grabbed her arm and started dragging her through the brush.

He pulled her through the overgrown, wet bracken to the boat, then through the sodden field to the tree line.

Farley had a lot to learn about Dexter Hughes!

27. TRIAGE

Everett hurried to help Mary Alice care for their friends. He found Avery and Geri but no one else. He called for Alice but got no answer. He knew something was wrong with the situation, but where was she? She would not have left her friends like this for anything. He needed to look for her, but the needs before him were extreme.

He climbed down to see if there was anything he could do to help Geri. If she was still alive, he could assure her that help was on the way. He could tell just by looking, Geri was badly hurt, but she would have to wait. He was more concerned with Avery's wound.

"Geri," he said. "Can you hear me? I know you hurt, but don't try to move. You're not bleeding badly, but you've probably got some broken bones. I promise you, help is on the way. We'll get you out of here."

Geri could only manage one word, "Avery," she half sighed.

Everett knew what she meant. He told her as briefly and truthfully as he could, "Avery is hurt but I think we got to both of you in time. I need to go help him now. You need to try to stay awake—and please, do not move. It will only make you hurt worse. Can you do that?"

"Yes."

"Help is on the way, Geri. Trust me."

"I do."

Everett quickly climbed out of the rocks. He could see Avery's wound needed immediate attention; his bandages were soaked with blood. All Everett could do until help arrived was to apply pressure and try to stop the bleeding.

By the time Billy, Harrison, and John got there, Avery was weak, but still conscious.

Bowser was badly hurt as well, but sensing the need, he had crept closer to his master. Avery heard the dog growl. It was the special growl reserved for John Wallace. *Funny,* he thought, *I might trust John with my life, but not with Geri.* It seemed strange that such clarity would find him at that particular moment.

Though he would not trust John with Geri, he knew John would do everything possible to get them home. John was the kind of man who made things happen whatever the circumstances. Avery let go then.

The doctor showed John and Everett where to apply pressure to stop the bleeding in Avery and Bowser. After assessing their wounds, he determined they could be safely moved without doing more damage to surrounding tissue. Both wounds would need further care as soon as they could get to better facilities.

After climbing down through the rocks, Harrison found Geri conscious and ready to try to stand. Her legs were okay, but breathing was painful, and she was dizzy. Harrison could tell from looking at the injuries, she had a broken arm, a probable concussion, and maybe some broken ribs.

It was decided. They would get Avery's boat and bring it to the water line at the edge of the rocks and load Geri from there. This would be painful, but better than trying to pull her up over the rough terrain without a litter to stabilize her injuries. They would get another boat for Avery and Bowser.

Doctor Windham had an office in town with room for a small clinic. Four beds were available, but seldom needed.

He did a careful examination of the three. Avery's and Bowser's injuries were more critical than Geri's, so Harrison did those surgeries first. He removed the bullets, applied the necessary poultices, and wrapped the wounds. It would take a while, but both man and loyal friend would survive.

Geri had a broken arm, some badly bruised ribs, and a raging headache. All would heal in time. The merciful doctor had given something to ease the pain after the examination. He sedated her now. She would not want to be awake while he set the bone.

He was washing up after setting Geri's arm, when Mary Alice returned to the forefront of his mind. She was missing. He had been greatly relieved when Josephine came through the front door at home. He believed Avery and Geri were the only ones in danger until he found them; then he realized Alice had vanished.

Doctor Windham had learned to distance his mind through medical training and practice. He was able to separate the unknown danger to his daughter from the desperate needs in front of him. He had kept the thoughts at bay for as long as he could. While one crisis was over, fresh anxiety and worry for Alice filled his mind. *Was there no end to the nightmare?*

28. TAKE CARE OF IT!

Dexter and Farley were not thrilled with each other. That was an understatement. The plan had gone wrong in *so* many ways. Now, rather than cutting their losses and escaping, to compound difficulties, Farley had taken another hostage. Dexter wanted no part of this.

The two vagabonds often picked up small tools as they thieved their way through the countryside. Dex was utterly disgusted with Farley. He got a shovel, threw it at him, and said, "You grabbed her—you take care of it! I'm out!"

Farley took the shovel.

Mary Alice heard the conversation and saw the gun. She could also recognize Farley. At that point she felt her life could be measured in minutes.

"Dear Lord, You *have* to help me!" her prayers continuing more earnestly now.

Though it was dark and she could not see very well, she could hear barking in the distance. It sounded like Jupiter. She knew Everett and her family would be out looking for her. She did not know where Farley was taking her, but she knew it was not good.

Earlier, when they were surveying the town, Farley noticed a half dug out pit that had probably been used as a root cellar. Before she realized what he was doing, he muttered, "What a waste." He immediately swung the shovel, slicing her scalp and forehead as he did.

Alice truly had not seen it coming, but she felt the hard, tearing edge of the shovel ripping and stinging as it sliced into her skin. She had never been around such violence. The force of the blow whirled her whole body around. She was momentarily knocked out as she fell beside the open trench.

Farley rolled her into the shallow pit with his foot. He quickly shoveled dirt and mud to bury her body. There were some old boards and brush nearby, so he hastily got those and threw them over the pit as cover. Thinking he was through for the night, he went back to the tree line. *Maybe Dexter would shut up now!*

There was no light when Alice opened her eyes. She was confused; she couldn't understand where she was. Her mind immediately went to the last thing she could remember, the shovel. *NO — she did NOT want to accept this!* Alice was covered in wet earth, bleeding and dazed, trying desperately to hold on to consciousness and sanity. She was a long way past fear.

She felt dirt fall loosely on her face where it was not packed tightly. She could feel a crawling sensation on her arms and neck, but she didn't have time to worry about crawling things. In other places, thick mud oozed or draped heavily over her body, holding her where she had fallen. *Oh dear, Lord,* she silently wailed in sudden torment. Her worst fear had become reality, *I've been buried alive!*

She needed to scream, but knew her mouth would fill with dirt if she did. She was very close to panic. In despair she cried out from her heart and prayed, *Dear God, You have to help me! Please Father, there's no one else,* she urgently begged. *Show me what to do. Help me get out of here.*

After a few anxious minutes of tears and near hysteria, she realized she had not died, *and* she could feel air wounding afresh the bleeding cut on her head. In the dark, Farley had not seen there were places where she was only *partially* covered. Then she remembered something her daddy had said, "Daughter, sometimes the only help you have is at the end of your own two hands."

She could do that, or at least die trying! She began to dig, slowly at first, and then new panic set in. Franticly, she clawed and dug until one hand broke through and found freedom. She continued the struggle, pulling debris away until she could wiggle out from under what would have become an early grave.

She sat up. Fresh tears came then. She was physically hurt and in pain, trembling with cold and fear, angry too, that anyone would do this to her. She was also grateful. Before she did anything else, she sat there in the hole and thanked God for sparing her life. The blow to her head could have killed her. Farley could have completely buried her and left her to smother. She shuddered to think about it and drew in an exaggerated breath just to prove she could.

Though she knew people were probably out looking for her, she also knew Farley could come back at any time—for what she couldn't imagine, but she was afraid he might. Her head was still bleeding and now hurt even more. She could already feel the stitches that were sure to come after the sting of cleaning the wound. She needed to get home. Alone, in tears of hurt and fear but thankfulness, she climbed out of the hole and started walking.

She was already wet from searching for Avery and Geri in the rain. Now she was muddy from head to toe. She was hunched over in pain, an apparition on the road, a shapeless, muddy blob.

Up ahead she could see two forms, one tall, one short. She couldn't tell who or what it was, but she didn't have the strength or will to run. The two figures halted. The blob fell from exhaustion.

There seemed to be something familiar about the apparition. A low growl turned to fierce barking as Jupiter ran forward to meet her. Behind him a voice asked, "Mary Alice?"

Everett could not believe his eyes! How could this mud covered, bloody mess be Mary Alice? What had happened to her? He picked her up and ran with her to his house. His mother got blankets while his dad got the car. Mary Alice closed her eyes and gave thanks again. She was going to be all right. Miss Irene cleaned Alice's face and comforted her as she would have her own child.

The McKenzies took Alice to her home where an anxious but grateful Vivian met them at the door. After seeing Alice's bloody head, she sent Billy to get Harrison from the clinic.

Alice felt better by just getting out of the heavy, muddy clothes. She eased into the bathtub. The hot water felt good to her bruised and aching body. Though there was pain in every movement, Vivian and Josephine helped her wash most of the mud out of her hair, careful not to disturb the gash on her scalp and forehead. She held a wet cloth over it until her father could look at the wound and clean it properly.

Bath finished, Harrison eased the hair of her scalp back, clipped the hair around the gash, and began the chore of cleaning the wound. This was going to hurt. He doused the area with an antiseptic like potion. The potion had a numbing quality and would ease some of the pain of the wound itself and the stitches that were to come. He then began to sew the beautiful face of his daughter. The country doctor possessed the skill of a plastic surgeon, his work always an art form. There would be no readily apparent scar. Only the painful memory of the ordeal would remain.

After they were sure Mary Alice would be all right, and there was no more they could do for the family, the McKenzies said good night and went home to their own bed. It had been a long, trying day for all.

Everett was worried about Alice. He decided he would stay with the Windhams and help watch over her. He said good night to his parents and went to the guest bedroom. Vivian thought this was a good idea because Harrison needed to be at the clinic in case Avery or Geri needed him.

Farley got almost to the tree line when he realized he had left the shovel beside the shallow grave. He had set it down to move boards and brush to cover the hole. He didn't have to think long to know Dexter would have another fit. Feelings between the two were already bad enough. Dex wouldn't need much more to make good on his threat to shoot Farley.

He thought about a lifetime of careless mistakes then. It actually felt like his whole life had been one long mistake. He was having a "moment." Sometimes he wondered about his thinking. It wasn't quite right, but he just didn't understand why. *Oh well*, he thought, *he would just go back and get the shovel. Dexter did not have to know about this latest lapse in judgment.*

Farley hurried to the spot where he had left the girl's body. It was empty of course, his prey was long gone. Dexter could not know this! Farley would get the girl and do the job right this time.

Mary Alice was restless at first, but then exhaustion took over. She was just about asleep when a rough, calloused hand covered her mouth, and a harsh voice whispered in her ear, "If you don't come with me, I'll kill everybody in this house." It was Farley. He had come back for her.

Petey went wild—cawing, screaming and beating his wings on the bars of his cage! Hearing the commotion, Everett thought Delilah was after the bird again.

"Mary Alice," he called, "Do I need to put the cat out?" No answer. He looked into her room, but her bed was empty. A breeze stirred the curtains at the window. He rushed to it in time to see Alice being pulled from the porch by a man.

As Everett rushed downstairs, he grabbed a small gun from the gun case.

He shouted, "Stop!"

They did. As they turned to face him, Farley held Mary Alice, clutching her. He would use her as a shield and drop Everett where he stood.

Everett was not going to allow Mary Alice to be taken so easily. In his haste, however, he had pursued right into Farley's hands.

Mary Alice had a searing headache, and she had had enough! She was not going farther.

She was standing slightly in front, but a little to the left of Farley, his arm around her, holding her. In his other hand he held a pistol aimed at Everett. Suddenly, with all her might, she elbowed Farley in the ribs, turned slightly out of his grasp, and kicked him, catching him in the knee. It was enough. Without a second of hesitation, Everett took the shot.

Dr. Windham was having a record night. The shot didn't kill Farley, but it put him out of commission. Harrison stopped the bleeding, packed and dressed the wound. The violent man could recover in jail while he waited for a state marshall to take him to a bigger facility in Nashville.

Farley would not come to trial in this county. In addition to the other crimes, he had made the critical mistake of trying to kill Geri, the only daughter of Judge Fitzpatrick.

Mary Alice needed desperately to feel safe again. Exhaustion was working on her; she needed to sleep. Her eyelids grew quite heavy as she settled again in her bed. This time, a sedative had begun its work. Everett was there too. He would be there for her, for whatever she needed. No new trauma would befall her. He would make sure of that.

29. EPIPHANY

Dr. Windham, Billy Russell, and John had been taking turns watching over Geri, Avery, and Bowser. It was John's watch; the others had gone home for sleep. The day had been long enough, and it was probably going to be an even longer night.

Occasionally, John stood and walked around just to stay awake. As he stood in the hallway of the clinic looking at the two beds, he noticed both patients were turned as though they were looking toward each other.

A growl came from under Avery's bed. Bowser yet lived, and as long as the dog had breath, he would not let John near Geri.

Finally, John had to admit it. The dog was right. As he watched them, the look, the tenderness he saw in their eyes for each other, it was too much.

He had lusted for the girl without ever caring for her. In that moment he felt something he had never felt before, shame. John was *consumed* with shame. He was filled with disgust for himself and loathing for every vile thought he had ever had and every suggestive word he had ever uttered.

Compared to what he saw in Avery's face, his sincere concern for Geri, John had nothing. He turned and walked away empty. As he settled in a chair to wait out the night, many things came to mind. He vowed to himself, things were going to be different.

30. MORE ANSWERS

Out in the barn, Henry Milton sat thinking. He heard footsteps behind him. Without looking he said, "Afternoon, John, I've been expecting you. I knew you'd be the one to figure it out."

John had been thinking about many things all night, Avery and Geri, clearing his father's good name, and the missing money. He came to a conclusion before dawn and spent the rest of the morning turning it over and over in his mind. It always came out the same. He knew the answer.

"Why, Henry, why did you do this?" John asked.

"I don't know," Milton began. "Maybe I resented all those years of just getting by for little or nothing, a pat on the back, or a free cup of coffee."

He went on, "Nobody sees me for who I am, John. I was a really good teacher. I've studied history, physics, math, and economics. By the way, this country is in for a very bad time economically. If you've got money in stocks, you need to think about getting it out."

The constable continued to explain how he took the money, "It was just too easy, John. I mean it was practically handed to me, the whole thing."

"I was helping Wallace carry in the money. He took a key from his pocket and opened the roll top desk. He opened one of the drawers and removed a false bottom. This revealed a note already under lock and key. He put the receipt for the train deposit and telegram in the drawer, then locked the desk, and slipped the key into his pocket. *That's* when it happened. The key slid down the leg of his pants to the rug. He never heard it hit the floor. I guess he was in a hurry or maybe just nervous about having so much extra money.

"Your dad was working with the lock on the safe, so I just took off my hat, laid it on the edge of the desk, and of course, it "accidentally" fell to the floor. That's when I got the key. Even if he saw me, he would only think I was picking up my hat.

"I hadn't thought about what I was going to do, but I knew I was going to at least read that note. It was important enough to hide, so it was probably important enough to read.

"Wallace put the money in the safe. I left him on the pretense of making my rounds for the night and locking up. While I was waiting at the jail across the street, I watched for him to leave the bank. It was getting dark, so being seen was not a problem. If anyone did, it would appear that I was only making my rounds".

The constable's recount of the incident continued. "Most folks in town don't know I have extra keys to several businesses just in case a key gets lost. I didn't really need his door key. If Wallace missed his desk key, he would think he had lost it somewhere. After using my extra bank key to get in, I opened the desk and read the telegram. It just informed Wallace of the deposit, fifty-thousand dollars. That's quite a haul! More than the telegram though, there was the other piece of hidden paper. It had the combination to the safe. As I said, it was handed to me.

"I quickly got the money, closed the safe and the desk, and I left. My wagon was a good place to hide the money, so I just threw some feed sacks and a tarpaulin over it and went back to make my nightly rounds. The situation couldn't have worked better if I had planned it. It was even a perfect night because a lot of the town's folks were going to Mary Alice's party.

"I wanted to mislead Wallace in the matter of the key. I threw it down beside his car on my way to the party. By morning light he would find it.

"There were no witnesses. Everyone was at the party, so I brought the money here and buried it under the hay.

"I knew it was wrong, but this was my chance to have something else in life, and I took it. The only problem now, John, what am I going to do with you? There's enough money for both of us you know. No one else has to know."

"No! It stops here. I've got to clear my father's name. I'll admit I've done some things I'm not proud of, but even I have a limit," John was emphatic.

"Well, I don't have any such high, moral compunction!" Dexter informed them. He had heard their conversation and now boldly stepped out from hiding behind the barn door with a gun in his hand.

Dex had been following the constable closely all day. He reasoned the constable would be the one to find the money, and when it was found, he would be there. He knew the money was missing because he and Farley had *also* robbed the bank. They had only managed to grab a few hundred dollars—there had been a demand for cash that day, and many bank customers had made withdrawals. Someone *else* had beaten them to the big money. They had found the vault door slightly ajar and left it the same way. The money they took was not enough to satisfy their greed. That's when they decided to watch the town and kidnap someone.

"I want the money, now!" Dex demanded. "Dig it up and hand it over. This is going to work out better than I thought." He motioned to John, "You, you're younger than he is, start digging. It'll be faster."

John began moving hay. Somewhere underneath the pile of Timothy and Lespedeza, there was fifty-thousand dollars. John and Milton knew the moment they handed it over, they were dead men. Dexter Hughes would think nothing of adding two more lives to the string of misery surrounding the money.

John was sweating, not from the work, but from fear. He needed time to think, time to formulate a deal, and he was running out of that precious commodity.

He knew the only possible way to deal with this man would be the lure of more money, a better deal. Slowly he started talking.

"You know, it's a shame I won't get to live to enjoy my inheritance," he said. He stopped and leaned on the pitchfork.

"You need to keep digging," Dexter urged, waving the gun.

"I just thought you might be interested in doubling your money. My way, everybody goes home happy." John was very good at baiting a hook.

Dex bit, "Okay, talk while you dig."

"You can have this fifty-thousand dollars and another fifty-thousand," John explained.

Milton looked worried. He had recently seen and learned so much about himself and people he thought he knew. The many twists and turns the whole thing had taken were beyond belief. *Maybe somebody should write a book. If he lived, he'd have plenty of time in prison*, he thought. At this point, that was more than he could hope.

John continued the deal. "Take us back to Dr. Windham's house. He has already offered to replace the stolen money, no questions asked. He believes my dad is an honest man, and that someone else took the money."

Dex shook his head in doubt. "It's gonna' happen? Just like that? You're gonna' ask, and he'll give it? I don't think so." He said this laughing and shaking his head. Though he realized John was trying to gain time and a way out of the situation, he found the deal to be tempting.

John continued to appeal to the man's greed. "He will, I tell you! You'll have one-hundred thousand dollars, and you've killed no one. There's no reason to start now. It's only money to him, just take it and go. We can all walk away from this a lot wiser."

The deal was not up to John's usual standard of finesse, but maybe it would buy them a few minutes. There were times in life when deals ran sour because of some lack of forethought. There had been *no* time to plan. At this point, all he could do was pray.

Dexter had no problem with killing. That was what he considered tying up loose ends. Fortunately, John had chosen his words well.

Dexter was greedy. One-hundred thousand dollars would get him far away, fast, and buy a new life. With enough money, anyone could start over.

"Alright," he agreed. Dexter looked at John for a moment as though in warning, "You know how this will end."

"Probably," he admitted. John did not want to think about that. All he *could* know was this—their lives were not going to end at that moment in a barn hall. That was enough for now.

Henry Milton did not like the way the situation had turned. It was one thing to endanger his life, but he never planned to bring harm to John and the others in any way. After seeing all the grief his own greed had caused, he wished he had never seen the money. John's family, the town—all had been good to him. He owed them. He decided right then it would end.

The three turned to leave the barn; Milton, followed by John, then Dexter with the gun. On the way out, Milton saw a short handled, grubbing hoe on a shelf near the door. He used it every summer for digging potatoes.

Unseen by Dexter, Milton carefully picked up the hoe and said, "If you don't mind, I'd like to close this barn door. The cows will come up for water and get out through the hall if I don't."

Dex smirked, "Yeah, sure, whatever," his mind already on the money.

Milton anxiously stood outside the door waiting for John to pass, the hoe in his hand. He knew he would only get one chance to undo the circumstances he had set in motion.

Dex could already see himself riding in a very long, black, shiny car through the night lights of a big city somewhere, anywhere but here. He just knew he was about to become a very rich man and couldn't wait to put miles between himself and this backwoods, nowhere town.

As Dex came out of the barn, Milton timed his swing perfectly. He swung the hoe at him, catching the gun. It went off, hitting Milton in the shoulder before it dropped to the ground. John, seeing the scuffle, hurried to help Milton wrestle Dex to the floor.

Something else had happened to John in the previous night. There had been the revelation of his relationships with Geri and Avery. His treatment of them had been so wrong, so selfish. They both had been real friends to him. They deserved better.

After that truth, came the shame of his intentions and behavior. The shame had made him realize at some point he had begun a life style that was completely out of character for what he truly wanted in life.

At home and at school he had been taught good business practices, but along the way he had learned to be ruthless when it came to making deals. He had become a man who would do almost anything to gain the advantage.

With matters of business, he had also been taught the value of honesty and ethical standards. He knew his parents wanted him to be successful, but they had never meant for him to give up integrity in the trade.

And more to the point, John knew right from wrong. He had gone to the little community church with his family most every Sunday. There he learned about real love and selflessness, the sacrifice of a heavenly Father pouring out for all mankind the righteous gift of His only Son's life.

John had left home to go to business school. Away from the influence of his family, he began to associate with people who had few morals and didn't care how they lived as long as they acquired exactly what they wanted in the moment. It was an easy way of life, pleasurable for sure. It was the kind of life that had made John a rich man materially, but poor in matters of the soul.

For some time now, he had felt a growing sense of wrong direction in his life. This weekend had been the culmination of his wandering.

He knew when to admit he was wrong, when to confess and ask for forgiveness. John had prayed as he had in childhood. Somewhere in his sincere admission and regret, he felt the weight of his sinful dependence on himself lifted, and in its place was love and peace. He had been forgiven. He could do no less now for Milton.

John tied Dexter's hands and feet and then put him in Milton's wagon. He looked at Milton's wound and said, "You're gonna' be a hero, Henry! We're turning the money in to the bank. Nobody will ever have to know what really happened."

Henry Milton could not believe what he heard. "Why would you do that, John?"

"Everybody deserves a second chance," John explained. "Mercy and forgiveness do a lot in a situation like this, and I believe you learned a lesson. I know I did."

Milton couldn't offer much but he offered this. "I was just gonna' run with the money, John. I never thought about what it would do to your family. I never dreamed the Windhams would be put through so much."

"I believe that's true, Henry. You can start over, just like you wanted, even without the money. You'll be a better man because of this."

Milton was sincerely humbled by John's offer. John could only guess what his words of forgiveness and encouragement had already done for the constable. He had learned much from the consequences of his actions. He was a changed man and would be forever grateful for John's mercy.

"Just get me to Dr. Windham. I'm not feelin' too good."

John wrapped the constable's wound and helped him get into the supply wagon.

When they got to town, John dropped Milton at the clinic. Next, he took Dex to jail where he was reunited with Farley. They would go to prison for a long time; the charges against them were many.

John then went to see his father and told him the whole story. Wallace Sr. was so relieved to get the money back, that he agreed he would not press charges against Milton. He also believed in second chances. After all, the man had risked his own life to protect John and keep the Windhams from further harm at the hands of Dexter. Wallace would go to Henry and offer his hand in friendship and forgiveness.

Rumors fly in small towns. Some heard that Henry had buried the money to prevent theft, captured a criminal, and saved John's life. Few ever knew the whole story, and by the time they did, it no longer mattered. Henry Milton proved to be a man of honor and was well respected by the whole community, even those closest to the situation.

31. PLANS

By Monday morning the town was back to normal except for those recovering from various wounds and injuries.

The clinic was full now. Bowser was enjoying the comfort of the third bed, and Milton was in the fourth. All patients were healing nicely.

The bank was open for business as usual. The money had been returned just in time for rail agents to transport it on to Birmingham. Vernon Wallace was glad it was gone!

Billy Russell had surprised everyone by offering to help out at the Benton's store. He knew how much they depended on Avery, but Avery was going to need time to heal. The Bentons needed Billy's help now, and would need it even more when Avery came home.

Billy's decision pleased everyone, especially Harrison. The offer to help had shown compassion and maturity on the part of his son, qualities he had tried to instill in all of his children. He was pleased with Billy.

By Monday afternoon, Mary Alice was getting restless. She did not feel well at all, but insisted on trying to get out for a little while. She and Everett were walking out on the patio when he suggested, "Why don't we get Billy to take us over to the island and retrieve your boat?" He really wanted to talk to her alone and this would give him the chance.

"No!" she said. "She could not do that yet; too much had happened there."

"How about a walk in Vivian's garden?" he continued.

That did not suit her either, too much sun.

Sensing there was something she had not told him, he patiently asked, "Is there anything in particular you would like to do?"

She looked at him, wondering if he could understand her fears. Would he say she was being silly? She knew Dexter and Farley could not hurt her, but still, there was a feeling of incredible vulnerability, a loss of control in her life. Like anyone else in her position, her feeling of security crumbled when she became a victim. She stood there not knowing how to begin. The right words would not come, so she began to cry.

Everett could see she was struggling and pulled her close. That did it! There in the shelter of his arms, all she had been through, both the beauty of her party and the brutality of the weekend came crashing through her emotions. Was it possible all had happened in just a weekend?

He kissed her head soothingly and whispered, "You're safe, Mary Alice. I'm here and you're in my arms. I will keep you safe—today and forever if you'll let me."

He looked at her for a moment more, unsure if he should go on. He had not planned to do it this way, but why not? He seated them both on the chaise and then dropped to one knee. "Mary Alice, I love you more than my own life. Will you marry me?" More tears from Alice.

She already knew the answer to that question, but she wanted to take a moment to examine her heart, to be sure. She tried to measure all she felt for this good man but found it was in no way quantifiable. She searched his face for some hint of insincerity. Seeing nothing there but truth, she said, "Yes," for she could not remember the beginning of her love for Everett. It was as though a fixed thing, unshakeable, boundless.

He kissed her passionately then in a long, slow kiss, careful of the bandage on her head. She gave no thought to the injury, though it was more than a little tender. She loved him with all of her heart, and she returned his passion.

They sat on the patio oblivious to everything except the love each felt for the other. Endorphins would be their anesthesia for a few moments. Absolute joy would keep painful memories at bay. Neither felt the need to rush the moment; moments this beautiful were too rare in life. There would be times when their faith in each other would be tested, hurtful times. Both would go back to this beautiful moment of clarity when they knew this was right, ordained, and therefore sacred.

32. SMOKEHOUSE SEASONING

All of the beans were broken now. The old woman needed to get a slab of bacon from the smokehouse and start boiling a piece of the meat. She would do that in a minute. It would simmer on the stove until tender, and then she would add the fresh beans and an onion. She would let the mess cook down a bit and add some fresh okra and a few small, new potatoes. Everything would slowly simmer until gravy developed. She could already taste her mother's recipe.

She went to the smokehouse for the meat, then on to the kitchen where she started the meat cooking, and then back to her chair.

She would just sit for a while now. The heat of the day was upon everything. Looking out at the trees, she thought about how some plants grew great or tall, and others, things like her ferns, were delicate, lacy or bushy.

There were other things too, poison vines, choking vines, things that needed ripping out by the roots. Some things needed killing, but everything, it seemed, had a purpose.

Many blooming plants became more beautiful from the direct heat of the noonday sun, others withered from its harshness.

While it seemed drastic to break off a thriving plant and throw away the coming flower, pruning would change the course of that plant, actually prolonging its blooming season and make it more beautiful.

A cooling breeze wafted up from the creek, bringing with it the scent of flowing water and the freshness of lush, green vegetation. Again she poured amber liquid over the ice, lemon, and mint already in her glass. She stared out into her gardens, drinking in both the tea and the beauty surrounding her.

The fragrance of the creek and the hint of mint lulled her back in time where she would finish her memory.

33. TRUST ME

John awoke much later than usual. Adrenalin levels had kept him from sleeping most of the night. Desperate to unwind before facing the day, he got up still uneasy about the events of the weekend, but more really, realizations about others and himself. Introspection can be a noisy thing.

He decided he needed to walk. Going out the front door today, he glanced at his reflection in the heirloom mirror, scoffed in disgust, and moved on.

Without thinking, he found he had walked to Jo's house. Vivian was gardening, "It helped her relax and gather her thoughts," she often said.

"Good morning, John. How's everyone at your house today?" She asked.

Somehow her question caught John off guard. "Much relieved," he acknowledged. "How are Mary Alice and Jo?"

"Alice is stronger than she looks. Her head will heal in time. Injuries to the soul take longer to heal. Everett is with her now; he's always been her refuge."

"Jo is different. She looks strong, but it's all on the surface. Inside, well, I worry about her," words of a mom.

"Do you think she would talk to me?" John inquired.

"I think she would. I know I would appreciate your trying."

John went in through the side door calling Jo's name. No answer.

He began climbing the stairs, still calling. He got to her room, knocked, and called "Jo," again, nothing. The door was slightly open, so he pushed it further. There, sitting up in bed, was Jo. She was staring at the wall, eyes pooling with tears, her face revealing the inner turmoil of shock, fear, and bewilderment.

John was sincerely overcome with concern for her. He walked over to the bed, settled beside her, and held one of her hands. "Jo, it's over, you're okay."

That seemed to register with Jo on some level. Her response was more tears. She wanted to, but she still could not speak.

He continued to soothe with words of assurance, just letting her get most of the emotion out of her system. He wasn't really sure of what to say. He knew a lot about women, but tears were definitely in "no man's land" because they could be produced by so many nebulous reasons.

Suddenly, he had a thought. He was not usually a spur of the moment kind of guy, but this idea had merit.

"Jo, you need to get out of here."

"No! I need to stay here for a while, maybe tomorrow."

"No," he gently corrected, "You need to get dressed, and then come outside with me and walk in Vivian's beautiful garden."

"No! I'm never going back in that garden!" she was adamant on this subject.

"Jo, you're safe. Your family is here with you. You don't need to be afraid anymore. It's truly over," he argued.

John saw this was going nowhere, and getting her out of the house would be much harder than he thought. He also realized Jo was in a worse mental and emotional state than he could imagine. He had another idea.

"How would you feel about taking a trip? We could drive to Nashville and stay at the Grayson Hotel; it's very impressive. You'd see lots of new things. We could drive up Saturday—eat, shop, and stay the night. It would get your mind off everything you've been through. Would you like to come with me?" he encouraged.

She thought for a moment. She knew John was right. She also knew she couldn't really live if she had to live in fear.

She spoke, "Mom and Dad won't hear of it. Mom will say it's not proper."

"Let me worry about them. You get up and get dressed. Go talk to your mother and Alice, pet Delilah. Do whatever you have to do to get to a better place mentally. Just take it one step at a time, and pretty soon, you'll be better. You'll see I'm right about this, trust me."

He stood up from the bed and threw back the covers. Taking both of her hands in his, he pulled her to a standing position.

"Jo," he said," look at me. Promise me two things. One, get dressed."

Though modest in every way, Jo was painfully aware she was standing with John in only her long, cotton nightgown and was a little embarrassed. John seemed to not notice, his mind already on arrangements for the trip. She quickly agreed to this, anything to restore some sense of propriety to the scene. "Okay," she promised. "I can do that. What's number two?"

"Promise me you'll go downstairs and join your family, that's all for today. They need to see you're coping in spite of all that has happened. It happened to them too you know."

She knew he was right again. "Yes," she said, "I will do that too."

John smiled then and said, "I'll come over tomorrow and check on you. I'll also talk to Vivian and Harrison about the trip."

"It won't do any good," she warned. "It would not be proper."

"But you'll go if they agree, right?"

She didn't actually have any hope her parents would agree to it, so she said, "Yes, I'll go."

John left Jo with a new purpose. He believed the trip would be just right, for both of them he admitted to himself.

After John left, Jo began her toilet for the day and was half dressed before she realized what had just happened. John had asked, practically begged her in fact, to go out with him. She was feeling better already. She sighed, *if only*. She knew her parents would not let her go.

Vivian was weeding by the time John came out through the garden doors. He sat in the shaded rocking chair and began. "Vivian, Jo is in worse condition than I thought possible. I wonder, could you and Harrison trust me enough, would you allow Jo to go with me next Saturday to Nashville? I know the conventions of the day scream a resounding *no* to this request, but I believe a short excursion would do her a great deal of good. I hope you consider me to be a close 'friend of the family,' and as such, I think convention would allow it."

She thought for a moment and said, "After what our two families have been through this weekend, I consider you more of a son, maybe a brother to Josephine. So yes, John, if you can get her out of that room and back to rational thinking, she may go. I'll speak to her father."

About an hour later Dr. Windham returned from seeing Avery, Geri, Henry, and of course, Bowser. It had been a good morning. Geri's mother and father, Judge and Mrs. Fitzpatrick had claimed Geri and taken her home to mend there. It would be a while before she took off on another adventure. Terrance and Corinne Fitzpatrick knew however, when Geri healed, she would be back to her old self. She couldn't help it. Adventure was just a part of who she was. No amount of scolding or warning would change her ways. They knew it and had accepted it.

Henry needed a little more care. He and Avery would remain at the clinic along with Bowser who was doing quite well. He just needed to be near Avery.

Harrison sat in the rocker on the porch while Vivian continued to pull weeds.

Harrison spoke, "I'm worried about Jo. How is she?"

Vivian knew an open door when she saw one. "I was talking to John earlier—you just missed him. Anyway, he has offered to take Josephine on a short trip to Nashville next weekend. A change of scenery would do her a lot of good. She would be with other young people, and she would have some fun. Lord knows she needs it."

"What are you suggesting, Vivian? They would go alone?"

"Yes, he will accompany her as a 'friend of the family.' That is acceptable isn't it?"

"Well, yes, but," he fumbled for words. "I don't know about this." He continued. "She needs the distraction, that's true enough, and I do trust John. He has proven to be a man of courage and standards. I guess I just wonder if this will reflect poorly on Josephine somehow. Will this encourage careless behavior on her part? If we allow this kind of freedom now, what's next? And besides that, Vivian, how will this action reflect on us, her parents? You know how people talk!"

"Harrison, we've taught all of our children right from wrong. They're good, responsible young adults. Let the girl grow up, it's time."

"Very well, I'll speak further with John about his plans."

"Good," she said. "He'll be here for supper." After saying that, Vivian went to the kitchen.

When Josephine came down the staircase for supper that night, she was again her beautiful self. All traces of fear had been replaced with hope. She was really looking forward to the trip with John.

Conversation around the dinner table was uncomfortable at first, everyone very cautious not to say anything to remind Jo of what she had been through, until Mary Alice came down the stairs to join them.

Alice was in a foul mood, which was uncharacteristic for her. She was sporting a huge bandage on her forehead that extended up into her hairline. Though she had taken a short nap, she looked grotesque from great, dark circles under swollen eyes. Her usually beautiful hair was a mess, sticking to the bandage in matted knots. It was just what Jo needed. She looked at Mary Alice, stopped eating, and began laughing.

"So glad I could be a comfort to you, Jo." Mary Alice said sarcastically. "Really, you don't need to be concerned for me." She leaned against the stair railing in real pain and more than a little self pity and whined, "My head still hurts!"

"I'm sorry, Alice," Jo offered, trying not to laugh, "But you could be the gross, disfigured, main character in a book of horror looking as you do."

"I know it! I'm going back to bed—not hungry anyway."

Alice turned to go back upstairs mumbling something about "concern in the family." She had to admit, she was not her usual sweet, sunny self.

"You should go back to bed Mary Alice. It's much too soon for you to be up. You'll be better tomorrow, you'll see. Let me know if you feel faint, dizzy, or sick to your stomach," the doctor told her. He thought for a minute.

Rising from his place at the supper table, the "daddy" in Harrison said, "Alice, honey, you've been through a lot both physically and emotionally." He went to her on the stairs, kissed Alice on her cheek, hugged her, and helped her back to her room. This was good because his tender response brought out the tears, expressing the fear and hurt she had been through the night before. Tucking Alice in as he had when she was a child, Harrison kissed her once more and said, "Rest now. Don't try to think about anything. Your mind needs to heal as much as your head. Your Mama and I love you very much, Mary Alice. With all my heart, I thank God you are safe."

As her dad turned to leave, Alice could only think about what a blessing it was to have such a loving family.

Harrison came back down to finish his meal and said, "John, Mrs. Windham tells me you're willing to escort Jo to Nashville. That's very kind of you. I would have suggested taking her myself, but with Avery, Geri, and Henry injured, I'd rather not leave town for a while."

"I'm glad you approve. I appreciate your confidence in me, and I'll be very careful to let nothing unpleasant happen to her. You have my word on that," John pledged.

Hearing that, Jo looked at her mother and rolled her eyes. The men were treating her as though she were a child.

Vivian cautioned Jo with a related look. Jo knew what that look meant. *If you want to go, let the men talk.* She knew she was perfectly capable of taking care of herself, but also knew her mother was right. Harrison and John both had good intentions, and this conversation was just their way of being in control of the situation.

Harrison did not like the idea one bit, but realized he had been out maneuvered. Too, the trip might be good for Jo. He might as well get on board with it.

John wanted to take Jo on the trip, but felt Harrison was right to be so concerned. He also knew he had better not mess up on this deal. Harrison would hold him responsible in every way for her safety and well being. What had he done?

He was not Jo's father, but he could be her friend. That, after all, was what she really needed.

34. EXCURSIONS

On the morning of their trip to Nashville, Jo dressed in a two piece, slim, gray suit with a lacy blouse under her jacket. Though she felt very stylish in new spectator heels, and was well pleased with her appearance, she already wondered if she should have bought shoes that were a little more comfortable.

John had been right. Just leaving town created anticipation for whatever was ahead. New interest already began to replace Jo's anxieties. There were small towns and sights along the way, things Jo had never seen. Conversation was not a problem either; each was at ease in the company of an old friend.

They arrived at the Grayson Hotel in Nashville by early afternoon. It had taken most of the day to get there.

The lobby of the Grayson was beautifully appointed in fine Italian furnishings of black, creamy white and pale gold; the theme carried throughout in rich marble. Massive ferns and graceful palms created intimate seating areas to encourage conversation among the patrons, while sumptuous fabrics invited them to linger. All of this led to the dining area, which in turn, led into the grand ballroom. Even from a distance, opulence was evident in the brilliant refraction of each tiny prism in the great chandelier. Though now only illuminated by afternoon sunlight, there were hundreds of spectrums of color dancing against the walls and ceiling.

John asked for two rooms, but was informed only a suite, two bedrooms with separate baths and an adjoining sitting room was available. Though not ideal for the sake of appearance, John reasoned it would be safer, and therefore preferable.

He could see Jo was favorably impressed with her surroundings, as was he. He tipped the bellman for helping with their bags and asked, "Jo, shall we get something to eat?" It was well past lunch, but too early for supper. Their breakfast had been very early and somewhat light.

"Yes," Jo replied. "That would be very nice. Then we can see what else we can get into."

A puzzled look passed over John's face. Quickly she explained, "I mean what else the Grayson has to offer, of course." John was relieved. For half a second he almost questioned how much he really knew about

Josephine. Would she prove to be a challenge away from the influence of home?

They took their time eating as they enjoyed Grayson's acclaimed chicken en croute, a salad of mixed greens, fruit compote with almond cookie, and iced tea. They both enjoyed the meal and agreed it was very refreshing.

On the way out of the dining area, John literally ran into an acquaintance from school.

Pearce Davenport was also leaving the lobby of the hotel. John really hated to do this, but manners necessitated introductions. Reluctantly John said, "Josephine, this is Pearce Davenport. Pearce, this is my neighbor's daughter, Miss Josephine Windham."

Jo extended her gloved hand and bid the man a cordial, "How do you do."

Pearce eagerly grasped her hand, looked into her eyes and said, "A great pleasure to meet you, Miss Windham." Then to John, "My, she is lovely!"

"And how are you, John?" He continued.

"Very well, thank you." John was eager to distance Jo and himself from this man although etiquette demanded a moment. "We were just on our way out."

"Great, I am too. I'll walk with you for a ways. Have you seen Nashville, Miss Windham?" He asked.

"No, not yet," she replied. "I think we're about to, the shops at least."

Pearce sensed he was intruding, so he excused himself saying, "I must go in the other direction. Perhaps I'll catch up with you later. It was a pleasure to meet you, Miss Windham, John, good day."

John nodded implying agreement. "Yes, we'll talk at length another time." He hurried to say, "Good to see you, Pearce," but there was no warmth in John's voice.

After the man left, Jo could see John's mood had instantly improved. "Take me shopping," she commanded.

"Yes, Ma'am," John agreed, "That's why we came!"

They went through all kinds of shops, jewelry stores, clothing, and shoe stores. It was all very exciting to Jo, but after a while, everything started to look the same. Exuberance for the sport was waning. She was tired, and her feet hurt.

"I should have known better than to try to wear these new heels all day. I wanted to look as fashionable as the other women here," she offered as an excuse.

"And you do, Jo," he hurried to agree. "Honestly, you look as though you were born for life in the big city, but I'm tired too." He went on, "Will you mind if we catch a cab and ride back to the hotel?" Knowing she wouldn't want to ruin his day by going in early, he took the excuse of fatigue on himself.

She saw thru his unselfish excuse. "No," she said, "I won't mind, and thank you."

They got back to the hotel and John decided he would look for a newspaper. Jo wanted desperately to go upstairs and rest for a bit, but more than anything else; she wanted to change her shoes.

"You go on up, Jo. I'll be along in a few minutes," John said, and hurried over to the front desk to look through several newspapers from larger markets than Nashville. This was a practice he had developed while living in the city, a means of staying ahead of the commodities market. He couldn't find exactly what he was looking for there, so he went back out to the street and around the corner to a large media vendor he had passed earlier. John began reading and completely lost track of time. After glancing at his pocket watch, he realized an hour had passed.

Jo had walked through the spacious lobby, and just as she got to the staircase, a friendly voice greeted her.

"Well, hello again, Miss Windham," greeted Pearce. "I was hoping I might run into you and John again before you left town. Where is John?" Pearce inquired.

"He's just getting a newspaper. He'll be along in a moment."

"I have some unexpected time," he pressed. "Would you care to join me for some afternoon tea here in the restaurant? We can watch for John, and he can join us. I'd like to talk with him about his plans now that he's finished school."

Jo was a little apprehensive, but reasoned that John knew this man. They were surrounded by other guests of the hotel and staff, and John would be joining them. She also intended to make the most of her trip. She said "Yes" to his invitation, turned with Pearce, and went to the hotel's café.

They ordered lemon icebox pie and tea, just as luscious as it sounds. Jo found conversation with Pearce both genteel and stimulating. This man had lived a bit daringly she thought, but seemed to converse comfortably within her social norms. He seemed to be a man equally at home anywhere from the countryside to a palace, very assured.

Pearce knew exactly what he was doing. The art of seduction begins with small steps, a gradual ease from the smallest "accidental" brush of the hand to embrace, the letting down of guarded instinct to blind trust.

"Have you been to Nashville before, Miss Windham?"

"No, I'm afraid this is my first visit. Please, call me Jo," she insisted.

"Thank you, Jo. I'm sure we'll be quite good friends. Tell me, have you seen very much of Nashville today?"

Jo had chosen to sit at a table that faced the opening to the lobby. She was enjoying the conversation with Pearce, all the while looking for John. "I'm afraid we only had time do some shopping. I'm sure we'll see more tomorrow before we leave." She knew polite conversation would only last so long, and then, if John did not show up, maybe she would feign a headache or something and excuse herself.

The minutes passed, ten, twenty, no John. By then she found Pearce to be charming, a southern gentleman by all accounts.

"Do you have family here in Nashville," she asked.

"Yes. My family lives in an area about five miles west of the town proper. I've a little sister about your age. You must meet her sometime. I'm sure you would have many things in common."

". . . I do wonder where John could be. Shall we look for him?" he asked.

"Maybe we should," she agreed.

They looked around the different areas of the lobby and went to the front desk to ask if he had been there.

The steward at the front desk, Albert, said, "Yes, he looked thru this newspaper stack for a while and left."

"Ah," Pearce said, "I'll bet he went to the corner. There's a large newspaper vendor there with many publications from around the world. He probably went there to read and just lost track of the time. It's just around the corner. Would you like to look for him? I could go with you, if you'd like."

By now Jo was anxious to find John, so she agreed again. They went to the vendor, but John was not there.

Pearce knew an opportune moment was at hand, so he said, "There are other places to look. My car is just there, across the street. Shall we look further?"

Jo knew she shouldn't, but she did not know how to say, "No, thank you," without seeming ungracious and insulting the man. After all, he was trying to find John.

"It's still early," he continued, "and we could be back, of course, as soon as you wish. I wouldn't want to alarm John if we should somehow miss him." Pearce knew he could only entice so far without seeming pushy.

Somehow the little bell of warning inside Jo's head did not go off. Maybe it was fatigue, the need to adapt to city ways, or the lack of worldly experience on her part. She did not see anything wrong with his suggestion.

"Thank you," she smiled. "But first I need to leave word at the front desk. If John returns, they can tell him I've gone with you. In that way, I'm sure he won't worry."

Pearce had to look away to hide his smile of satisfaction.

John, seeing how much time had elapsed, hurried back to their suite at the Grayson. Maybe, he hoped, Jo was taking a nap. She wouldn't notice the time in that case. If she did notice the time, he was in big trouble!

"Jo," he called softly, "I'm back." No answer. *Where would she be*, he wondered, immediately anxious? He should check with the front desk. Perhaps she had left a message.

"Yes, Sir," answered Albert, "Miss Windham left this note for you."

John,

I'm with Pearce. Ran into him, waited in café, then wondered what happened to you.

Gone to check newsstands. If you're not there, we'll be back soon. Don't worry.

Jo

John's mind echoed, *don't worry!* Harrison would kill him quickly, no worry about that. He had trusted John to take care of Jo, and he hadn't.

John knew the kind of man Pearce was. He had run with him some in his younger days before he found out how awful Pearce could be. John knew him only too well. Already anxious for Jo's safety, he ran into the street to his car.

Pearce drove to several corners "looking" for John, getting a little farther from the hotel with each turn. He began by asking, "Jo, would you mind if we stopped here? John may have met other, mutual friends, and since this is a place we used to visit on occasion, they may have come here for a friendly drink."

The hole Pearce now called a bar did not look like a place John would ever visit. Certainly, she had never been in such a place, but what was she to do? Jo could see she needed to think a little faster because things had already gone farther than she wanted. "Why don't you go in and check," she said. "I'll just stay here in the car and wait—if you don't mind."

Pearce went in and stayed until Jo couldn't imagine what was taking so long.

Reluctantly, she summoned her courage and went into the bar thinking—*if Mother ever finds out . . . well, that must never happen!*" She found Pearce, playing cards and drinking. No, he was on his way to being roaring drunk!

Silence fell on the room as she stood in the doorway. These patrons were not accustomed to the presence of a lady, especially a young woman so pretty and obviously ill at ease in her present surroundings.

Pearce was the kind of man who enjoyed being bad. He laughed at her, seeing the confusion and discomfort clearly on her face. Sneering at her he said, "It's about time you came in here! I want you to meet my friends," He laughed again, this time at himself for the use of the word "friends." These were no friends. They were the worst of a sort, and none could be trusted for anything.

Alcohol truly brought out the bad in Pearce. He stared at Jo until his eyes grew narrow as if trying to assess her. He mocked her again, for he suddenly took offense at her virtue and innocence. "Your beauty doesn't quite fit this place, Miss Josephine." She was beautiful, true enough, but more. She had an uncommon virtue, goodness, something he would never have. Self hatred is a most destructive thing. He was full of loathing for the thing he had become and his so called friends. "Take a good look, boys! You won't find many like her." All eyes fell on Jo, leering at her, for these men lacked morals and decency. These men detested themselves too, for they knew they would never possess anything so precious and beautiful. The most they could hope for was to enjoy her torment. They would tease and taunt for they were seasoned in ways of cruelty. Pearce raised his glass and sarcastically said, "To the appreciation of beauty my friends!" The rough, howling laughter she had interrupted began again.

Poor Jo actually believed she had a choice. "Pearce, I'd like to go back to the hotel now, please," she said softly.

"We'll go back in a bit," he slurred. "What's the hurry, Miss Josephine?" he mocked. "You need to loosen up." Saying this, he poured a drink for her and shoved it across the table. "Here!" he commanded. "Drink it!"

Jo was indignant now. "Very well, is there a man among you who will take me back to the hotel?" she pleaded.

A voice from the corner yelled, "Yeah baby, I'll take you!" At that remark, the whole bar erupted in laughter at her expense.

Embarrassed, Jo turned and left. She would only get further grief from this crowd.

It was getting dark now. There was no question about it; she would have to walk back to town. *Why had she worn these shoes?!!*

Presently a car drove by, turned around and headed her way, slowing as it neared. *"Now what?"* she thought.

John stopped the car. "Get in," he ordered.

She knew what he was going to say, dreaded hearing it, but she was not stubborn enough to keep walking.

"What were you thinking?" He demanded, sounding a lot like her father.

"You said he was your friend!"

"Not friend, acquaintance! I knew him two years ago. He's a womanizer, a cad, and a drunk!"

"You could have told me!" she protested.

"I didn't think you'd run off with the man! You just met him."

The argument continued. "It wasn't like that. We started out looking for *you*," she reminded.

"And he used that as an excuse to get you alone, Jo!" He softened. "You couldn't know that," he admitted. "I don't mean to fuss. I told your parents I'd take care of you, but I'm going to need a little help. Big cities are quite different from home. You can't trust everyone. There are a lot of things to enjoy here, but also people who would hurt you.

The people who live here are accustomed to judging one another. They know what to look for, the signs which tell if a person can be trusted or not. You don't know those things because you've had little experience with that. Please, just do as I ask and stay close," he begged.

She knew he was right. Her lack of forethought and inexperience had just about trapped her. *Oh well,* she thought, *so much for relaxation and getting away from my fears.*

John breathed an audible sigh of relief. She was safe, that's what mattered. He had said enough and did not want her to feel undue guilt. The trip could still be salvaged; he truly wanted her to enjoy it.

"Friends?" he asked.

Jo hated what she had put John through. "Yes," she said, "I won't do anything like that again, I promise."

They drove in pleasant silence then for a moment or two when John asked, "Well, Jo, it's early yet, what would you like to do?"

She thought for a moment, "We could—John, look out!" Jo braced herself for the crash.

They were little more than a mile from town when a deer from a nearby cornfield bolted in front of the car. The warning came too late. John swerved just in time to miss the deer, but ran off the road into a ditch, the undercarriage of the car coming to rest among roots from large trees and brambles.

John could not believe his luck this night, or rather the lack thereof.

He knew better than to ask if anything else could go wrong! "Are you alright, Jo? Are you hurt?" he asked, quite concerned. He had seen her fly forward, almost hitting her head on the dashboard. Fortunately, they had not been going too fast, and she had had time to use her arms to shield against the coming impact.

The car was tilted over on the passenger side. John hurried around to Jo's side of the car, but before John could reach her side, she slid out the door and fell into a thicket of brush and blackberry vines. The thorns of a nearby bush caught her lacy blouse and tore it. She tried to escape the hold of the brambles and ripped her skirt. He helped her out of the bushes and continued to survey for injury. John could see only scratches and ruined clothing. Otherwise, she was not hurt.

He helped her cross the ditch and step up, onto the road. Stepping awkwardly on the hard, packed surface, she broke the heel of a shoe.

"That does it! I don't think I can take one more moment of *relaxation* in this place!" She started to cry.

Though a natural impulse, John knew not to laugh at the situation, but some things were just beyond belief. He stifled the grin and pulled her close to his side. Holding her there he said, "Jo, I'm so sorry for everything. This is not the trip I planned. We're okay." He continued, "We're just going to have to walk a little. It's only about a mile to town. I would walk and leave you here, but you wouldn't be safe. Please stop crying," he urged.

Pausing a moment, he thought and said, "I can solve one of your problems. Here, give me those shoes."

Reluctantly, she did as he asked and gave him the shoes. "I doubt you can fix them."

"Jo, some things are more painful than they're worth." Saying this, he tossed them over his shoulder into the woods without ever looking back.

She was beginning to marvel at this man. "Thanks," she said. "I should have done that a long time ago!" They both laughed then and started walking toward town.

Very few cars were on the road now. Most people seemed to be in for the night. They heard a car coming from behind them, and from the sound of the engine, it was going too fast. Jo and John turned in time to see a car full of drunks from the bar, still laughing and jeering, and it was headed straight for them. They jumped aside just in time for the car to pass, the rowdy laughter ringing in Jo's ears. This seemed a cruel joke to her, even if it was only meant to scare them.

John was unmoved. He had learned some time ago that people could be mean, especially if they were frustrated by the circumstances of their own lives.

"We need to keep walking, Jo," he said calmly.

They were about to go, when another car came and stopped beside them. This time it was Pearce. He had sobered some and stopped to give them a ride. "You might as well," he reminded them, "It's better than walking."

Jo opened her mouth to tell Pearce exactly what she thought of him, when John gave her a warning look that said, *this is not the time*. She heeded the look and closed her mouth.

"Thanks," John said, "but you need to let me drive. We might not get very far in your condition."

"Do you always have to be so righteous?" Pearce asked accusingly. "Oh—alright!" Pearce crawled into the back seat knowing he was to blame for the situation. *He knew he could drive home without a problem, but it wasn't worth an argument. John was such a know-it-all!*

They rode in silence until they stopped at the Grayson. Pearce got out with them and asked, "John, would you like to get a drink for old time's sake? No hard feelings, Okay?"

John helped Jo out of the car, then turned to Pearce and said, "Right, no hard feelings!" Then he slugged the one time acquaintance with his fist, knocking him onto his butt.

"Never come near me or this woman again!" John warned.

They turned and walked into the lobby of the fashionable hotel. John's clothes were torn, and his hands were scratched and bleeding from the bushes at the wreck and from hitting Pearce. Jo looked even worse. Her lacy blouse was torn from the rough bushes as she climbed out of the car. Her suit was dirty and ripped, and of course, she was barefoot. She held her head high as John took her arm and escorted her through the lobby as if nothing were amiss. On the way by the front desk, Albert looked at them and started to speak. John stopped him mid sentence with an exhausted look and said, "Don't ask!"

They were once again safe behind the doors of their suite. Too tired to have much of a discussion, John turned to Jo and said a bit sarcastically, "I trust you'll be here in the morning?"

She rolled her eyes only slightly, and agreed, "Yes, I'm sure I will." She caught displeasure from his tone, but knew she deserved the remark.

"Then we'll have breakfast together. Good night Jo."

"Good night, John. I do appreciate everything you've done for me," she added sincerely.

John went into his bedroom, got cleaned up, and started thinking. He went back to Jo's door and whispered, "Jo, are you asleep?"

"Yes. Go away." she answered, keeping her eyes shut.

"Can we talk?"

"No, I'm tired," *If he would go away, I could be asleep in half a minute,* she thought.

"Please, Jo."

"Oh, all right!" She got out of bed and came to sit with him on the couch.

"Look, I'm sorry. This has not been the trip I wanted it to be," John said. "It's just that I was terribly worried about you."

"Yes, I know, and I didn't mean to scare you. Things just got out of hand before I knew what was happening."

"I tried to tell you about Pearce. He hasn't changed from when I knew him two years ago. He seemed decent enough at first, and we enjoyed the same circle of friends. After a while I began to see his business dealings were less than honorable. In social situations, I saw how he treated women, and how he acted when he got drunk. I resolved to have little or no contact with him after that, though I did not make an issue of it."

"Besides," he went on, "had you been here, I wanted to take you to supper. Jo, you're a beautiful woman." He brushed back a stray curl, and then touched her face. He looked at her as though wondering about something, and before she knew it, he leaned in and kissed her.

For Jo, the whole night had seemed like a crash course in how to survive strange situations and emotions. While she was coping in some areas, she was panicking in others. This was a new kind of panic, not from fear as in the kidnapping or harmful situations, but panic because she realized he was going to kiss her again; and he did. It was soft, warm, and full of passion, just like the man.

He seemed to remember they were alone, pulled her close, and whispered, "You better go back to your room. Good night, Jo, and sweet dreams."

Jo was suddenly having the best night of her life! And he wanted her to dream? Fat chance of that happening! She would be awake all night just thinking of John and that kiss. She knew he was right though. "Good night," she said and closed the door to her room.

The next day was Sunday. John got up early and made arrangements for his car to be towed. He also sent a telegram to Harrison, telling him about the deer and the mishap with the car. Everyone was fine, but they might have to stay longer if the car could not be driven.

When he got back to the suite, Jo had dressed in a pretty, green floral dress and was in high spirits. Fortunately, she had also brought her regular, Sunday shoes, lower heels in a neutral cream color. He took her to breakfast as promised, and they were ready to see Nashville.

On their way out of the hotel, Jo noticed a very well dressed man getting in an expensive car with a driver. "Who is that?" she ventured aloud.

"You don't want to know him," he answered. "He has money, but no scruples."

"How would you know that?" she teased.

"I used to live here, remember?"

"Oh. Who is he? What do you know about him?"

"Let me show you Centennial Park and the Parthenon, and I'll tell you everything."

When they got to the park, she couldn't wait. "Alright, who is he?"

"His name is Jeremy Thornton Craig. He is very wealthy, but he got his money by questionable means. He was just a homeless boy who got his start by carrying whiskey through the hill country for moonshiners. Later, he made and sold his own brew."

"He moved on to being the brains behind a small-time theft ring, but he knew if he wanted really big money, he needed the appearance of propriety. He went to business school, where he learned to engage in legitimate business, but chose to swindle innocent people out of their hard earned money. He ruined several good men with get-rich-quick schemes. The last I heard of him, he had moved on to even bigger things.

"His specialty now seems to be getting to know how a company works, move in, and manipulate the owners to get what he wants. First, he looks for a company with a reputation for cutting corners. He learns their secrets, both professional and personal. He then threatens to share the information with the highest bidder. To put it in a word, it's "blackmail".

"The man you were with last night is almost as bad as this man."

Jo sat there speechless. She could not imagine such dealings in her own small community. But a week ago she could not have imagined any of the events of that weekend either. *What was the world really like,* she wondered? She shook her head in disbelief and asked again, "How do you know him?"

John hated to own up to it, but he went on. "I came very close to a business deal with him once, but at the last moment I backed out. Something about the man made me uneasy, and I just had a feeling it wasn't a good deal. The man who took my place in the deal, the man Jeremy ultimately cheated, was found floating in the Cumberland River. No one knows if he fell, jumped, or was thrown to his death. He left a wife and three small children with no means of support.

"If Jeremy has a conscience, it doesn't show. He walked around town as though absolutely nothing had happened. There was never any proof of wrong doing. He was never charged with anything.

"Bad things seem to parallel the man. He's never in the middle of trouble, but he's never far removed either."

Jo sat there silently for a while then said, "Our families have been so blessed. You're a good man, John."

His reply, "I've been lucky! I've had the same opportunities to get into trouble, and I almost did a few times. Always something made me walk away. It's like a voice in my head, behind me maybe, telling me which way to go."

"Just when I think I've got you figured out, you surprise me, John."

"Not half as much as you surprise me," he laughed. "Are you ready to go?"

"I think so."

"Good. Let's rent a carriage and have some fun."

They drove back through town passing the State Capitol and went on to the early site of Fort Nashborough. Next, they stopped for a while to watch the barges move freight on the Cumberland River. On both sides of the river they could see industries and businesses that would provide jobs needed for growth in the bustling town. Leaders were emerging in all areas that make a town great; the business sector, politics, culture, religion and society, but none could imagine the city of old fashioned charm would later become the jewel called, Nashville.

They enjoyed the ride and got out of the carriage at the Grayson. Jo went upstairs, thinking a hot bath would be relaxing before supper.

John wanted to get a newspaper and enjoy it with a cup of coffee in the hotel lobby before he came up to their rooms. He reasoned that would give Jo some extra time to dress before dinner, and said he would be upstairs in about twenty minutes.

She drew her bath and enjoyed it. She casually put on her robe while humming to herself, for she had finally begun to relax and enjoy the trip. Hearing John in the other room, she called out, "John? I'll be dressed in about fifteen minutes. Will that be okay?"

The double doors to her room opened. Jo's breath caught in her throat as she gasped in anxious surprise.

Pearce Davenport stood in the doorway with a mocking smile, "Take your time," he said. "We've got all night."

Jo stood there, her face distorted with confusion. "Pearce—how did you get in? Why are you here?"

Pearce smirked, "Honestly, you can't be that naïve. I've come to finish our business from last night of course," laughing as he said this, just to see her discomfort and fear. "Besides, I owe John for hitting me," Clearly, he was already bent on a plan of revenge.

"John will be here any minute," she warned.

"In that case, you had better get dressed."

"And if I don't?" she opposed.

"Then I'll drag you out of here dressed as you are."

Seeing she needed further persuasion, he drew a small gun from the pocket of his jacket. Jo stepped back, turned to get her things, and returned to the privacy of the bath to dress.

She waited as long as she could, praying John would return. That didn't happen. Pearce gave her five minutes, opened the door and said, "Let's go." He continued, "Go along with me and maybe you'll be back by morning. If you scream or try to alert anyone, you'll be responsible for whatever happens to them, so don't try it!"

Pearce led her to the street, where a waiting car drove them toward the river.

Finishing his coffee and paper, John returned to their suite.

"Jo," he called, "are you ready?" No answer. *This will just not do!* He had trusted her to be where she said she would be. She had promised she would not leave. Where was she? Maybe she had taken the stairs instead of the elevator and he had missed her. He would go check with the front desk before he had his fit!

There was no message, but the bellman had seen her leaving, being pulled rather, by Mr. Davenport. John knew instantly, Jo was in trouble, and this time, not of her doing. He raced out to the street to hail a taxi, anxious to check the usual haunts Pearce frequented. He went back to the bar where they had gone the night before and found no one. John could think of only one other place, and he would rather not think about that. It was down on Second Avenue near the river.

John knew he would have to slip in from the back door because it was Sunday night and the bar was supposed to be closed. The lawless, filthy place had not changed. It was still filled with acrid smoke and a vile odor that only grew worse as he looked for Jo. There was no crowd tonight, only a few shiftless drunks who were lounging, sipping, and hoping for a free drink, an old hag of a woman sleeping in the corner, and some men who had paid for a bottle. All were trying to forget the misery in their lives. If Jo was here, they would be on their own.

John did not see Jo or Pearce when he entered the place, so he walked through the bar to the back room. There was usually a card game in the hall, but not tonight. He stood by the door listening to the steady rhythm of thump, then five or six steps. Again, thump, then five to six steps.

He recognized the sound. Pearce was practicing with his knife. Rather, Pearce was terrorizing and tormenting Jo by throwing a knife in the direction of her head. John had seen this tactic before.

He could feel anxiety and tension mounting, knowing it was possible, just by opening the door, their lives would be changed forever. What else could he do? He had to do it.

John found her there, sitting, tied to the chair. Her face was streaming with tears, and her eyes were full of fear. He suddenly realized she was staring at something behind him.

"Evening, John. You're quick. I thought it would take you longer to find me."

With that remark, Pearce again threw his Bowie knife at Jo, missing her by inches. She fell for it. Completely terrified, she could only squeeze her eyes tightly shut and cry into the gag in her mouth.

John knew Pearce was a man who enjoyed drama. He also knew without turning around, Pearce had a gun pointing at him. He had used Jo to lure him there to kill him. Revenge had always been a big thing for Pearce. He would ravish Jo, and then kill her, too.

No time to think this one through. John would get only one chance, and their lives depended on it. He heard the hammer of the gun click before he could turn around. Everything happened quickly then.

Pearce shot first. Then, there was a second shot. Jo did not understand. Her mind was in a state of heightened fear and terror. John seemed frozen, very still. She could only imagine what she would see as he fell, his body lifeless in an ever expanding pool of blood, but there was nothing. She forgot to breathe. The only sound she heard was the audible gasp of her own breath as Pearce's gun fell to the floor, then Pearce.

Most people did not know this about John—he always went armed in big cities or had something very close by. It was only one of a few habits he had taken up while living in Nashville.

John had held the small gun in his right hand, low, close to his body. As he turned to face Pearce, he had raised his hands as if in surrender and fired. Pearce did shoot first, but it went wide. He fell without ever knowing what had happened, the gun in his hand hitting the floor before he did.

The shots brought the bartender into the room. One look at Jo told him all he needed to know. She was still gagged and tied to the chair. Pearce and the gun rested just as they had fallen.

John hurried to Jo, quieting her tears with soothing words, holding her in his arms to still her shaking. He untied her, while the bartender sent for the police. By the time they arrived, the bar was closed except for John, Jo, and the bartender.

Though she was in a state of shock, Jo was able to retell the whole story starting with the night before. She had been terrorized by the man, but she managed to tell the events of the evening without crying. John was proud of her for controlling her emotions, but he knew they would come out later. They had to. No one could endure what she had and not be affected by it.

Though there would probably be an inquest later, Pearce's family would insist on that, the police would not press charges. Clearly, it was a case of self defense. Intent to do bodily harm was there. The girl had been taken at gun point, held by restraint, terrorized, and used as a ploy to do further harm to John. John had been fearful for both lives and acted as any other person would have under the circumstances. Maybe he *should* have gotten the police before looking for Jo. Maybe they *could* have stopped Pearce. But what if they had been too late to save Jo? Second-guessing was pointless.

There had been other accounts of harassment and retaliation concerning Pearce Davenport. Men like him were all alike. They would continue to be a menace to society until the day they went too far. Someone, the intended be victim usually, would be forced into a situation with no way out. The victim would have to try to defend himself or be killed. There really was no other way.

The police gave Jo and John a ride back to the Grayson. Again, Albert considered their appearance, but asked no questions.

It was quite late now. Guests of the hotel had gone to bed. The lobby was empty except for Karl, the doorman, and Albert.

John's eyes went to the hotel's coffee service just inside the café. It was closed for the night, but in a lavish resort like the Grayson, it would be completely stocked at all hours with whatever anyone would need for a perfect cup. They both helped themselves. John only wanted good, honest coffee, the flavor rich and deep, comforting. Jo however, needed milk, a lot of milk and sugar, "Yes, please."

They carried their coffee to the elevator and waited for a car, each saying nothing, trying to make sense of all that had happened. It would be a long night. First, they would have to get over their shock. Though wanting to calm down, adrenalin was still coursing throughout.

They sat on the couch looking like a pair of rough, worn, old shoes. Each was staring at the elegant but empty fireplace, coffee in hand. They sipped slowly.

Jo was the first to move. She could see John was visibly affected from having to kill the man. Anyone would be. Setting the coffee aside, she began to relax and leaned her head against John's shoulder. As if reading his mind she said, "John, you had to shoot him."

"I know—but that doesn't make it easy or right."

She went on, "You don't know what he was planning to do to me!"

"Yes, I do!" He looked at her earnestly as he said this, "And after *that* he would have killed both of us and thrown our bodies into the river."

The warm milk in the coffee and exhaustion began working on Jo. She closed her eyes for what she thought was just a moment.

John sat very still until he heard her breathing deepen. He kissed her head then, covered her with a blanket, and left her sleeping on the couch.

He needed to be alone tonight, too much had happened. He had never killed a man. He felt sick to his soul. Without turning on any lights, he crawled into the middle of the bed, keenly aware the burden of guilt was growing, and if it continued, the weight would crush him. He was sure of this.

He fell on his face and cried, "Oh God, help me! I can't fix this and I can't bring him back." As tears of regret fell, he knew all the tears in the world would not change the events of the night. He grieved for what he had done, he was a tortured man. "I know I'm not worthy, Lord, but please, forgive me and 'Restore the joy of Thy salvation . . . .'" (Psalm 51:12 KJV.)

He had physically done all anyone could do in a no-win situation, and it was not enough. Mentally, he knew he did not have a choice. He had to stop Pearce.

John was grateful they were alive, but emotionally, he was filled with anguish for taking the man's life. Now he brought the matter to the only One who could pour the healing balm of forgiveness over his soul. Deep contrition felt, absolution given. He continued in prayer until he had exhausted his grief completely and fell asleep.

Jo awakened sometime in the night. A prayer for John was also in her heart. "Dear Lord, John needs to feel Your presence surrounding him, holding him. He needs to feel Your love and forgiveness. Please, Father, help him find mercy and peace, and help him to forgive himself."

She continued, "Father, I thank You for taking care of us through this awful night. When I was alone and afraid, You were there with me. When Pearce was threatening me with the knife, You heard every word he said and my every, tortured cry. You alone saved me by letting John find me in time. I thank You for sparing my life. Now please help John, dear Father, bless him and give him the forgiveness he desperately needs for what has happened. Help him to see he did the only thing he could do. Help us to go forward from this and live lives that honor You."

She felt a need to check on John. Finding him asleep, she slipped back to her room. The night had been awful, but somehow they had lived through it. Jo closed her eyes again. This time she slept, for this time she would dream of home. Both she and John rested then, in the hands of Mercy and Grace.

John awoke around six the next morning. He immediately looked for Jo. She had been through so much. *Was it possible*, he wondered? *Yes.* He knew. *He loved this girl.* He didn't know when it happened. *Maybe it was the sight of her crying in the rose satin dress.*

The events of yesterday came quickly to mind, but instead of sorrow and guilt, he found he was really grateful to be alive. *Yes, he was grateful!*

So many memories from childhood had flooded his mind in the night, remnants of scripture actually. The verses that helped the most were from the book of Psalms. He remembered many, one in particular:

"Many sorrows shall be to the wicked; but he that trusteth in the Lord, mercy shall compass him about." (Psalm 32:10)

Today, John was a new man. He had things to do! But first, he thanked God for His mercy and forgiveness.

He left Jo still sleeping and went down to Fifth and Broad to the garage to check on his car. It was ready; no major damage had been done. The axle was not broken, and the dented bumper had been straightened. The paint could be fixed later.

Next, he stopped at a dress shop. *Jo could not go home looking like that!* Besides, who ever heard of going on a shopping trip and buying nothing? He needed to shop for an alibi if nothing else and he needed to do it now. There would no other time before the trip home. *Jo's best suit was in tatters, and her shoes were somewhere in the woods.* He laughed at that memory. The dress she was sleeping in, the green, floral, was wrinkled and stained from the filth of the bar. She had been in that dress in a hideous situation. She had slept in it, and he was sure she would like to burn it and forget all that had happened.

He chose a simple white cotton blouse with a V-shaped neckline and wide collar. To go with it, he happened to see a slim skirt in a beautiful, jewel tone of golden brown. Copper, the salesgirl had called it. She suggested a wide, matching ribbon for Jo's hair to bring the ensemble together. He could already see Jo in his mind, hair just so.

A shoe store was next in line, so he went in. He knew he was in over his head on this, but he would do his best. Guessing at the size needed, a pair of smart heels caught his eye. They were similar to the pair now in the woods, but prettier, and would match the skirt perfectly.

He was almost back to the Grayson when he passed a jewelry store. There, in the window, was the last of his treasure hunt. He really didn't know he needed it until he saw it. It was an heirloom cameo in shades of cream and rich brown. The delicate stone was edged in a carving of fine Italian gold. It's matching chain glittering, caressing the stone, iridescent, like water in a stream in the sunlight. He was impressed.

His image of Jo was getting clearer. He glanced at other things and decided not. It was still too early in the relationship.

When he got to the suite, it was only about ten o'clock. "Rise and shine," he cheerfully greeted Jo.

She was definitely not a "morning person". She greeted him with a scowl. In the light of morning, she was even more of a mess than he remembered. Her hair was a bush, and her eyes were swollen. Her twisted, wrinkled, cotton dress now gapped open where it had lost a button.

"Jo, dear, please go to the sitting room and see what I have for you."

Reluctantly, she obeyed. She couldn't believe her eyes. John was truly amazing! She would never have believed a man capable of such a feat. Her father stayed away from anything remotely related to shopping for the women in his family. She was thrilled with everything, and surprisingly, everything fit! It almost bothered her that he could size her up so accurately.

She came to the cameo and sat down, stroking the beautiful thing in her hand. John had given her so much. Things to be sure, but more, he seemed to understand the needs of her heart. She knew she would remember this moment.

He sat beside her and urgently asked, "Do you not like it? Is it not right?"

"It's so much more than right, John. It's perfect! Thank you," she said, and kissed him. The kiss was perfect too, soft, sweet and sincere.

"You need to get some coffee and enjoy your newspaper while I get cleaned up," she urged. He did as he was told.

He was just finishing the second cup and the paper, when she came out of her room after getting dressed. She was exactly as he had envisioned from head to toe.

Her beautiful brown hair was caught low against the nape of her neck with the copper ribbon draping gently over her shoulder and against her back.

The crisp, white blouse fit neatly into the trim skirt. It was the newest style, a little shorter to reveal the shoes.

"Here," she said, holding out her hand. "Help me with the necklace."

"Let me look at you first, Jo. You're stunning!"

As he fastened the clasp, he couldn't help but notice how good she smelled. She turned to him and said, "Thank you, John," with all earnestness. "Everything is truly beautiful." Smiling, she kissed him again. He held her close and began to feel something else tugging at his soul.

He wanted to say something it seemed, but the time was not right, and he did not know how to say it.

Instead he asked, "Well, are you ready to go home?"

"So ready!" she replied.

There wasn't much for Jo to pack. John had cleaned up, changed clothes, packed, and read the paper while Jo dressed.

They stopped in the café for a quick bite before the long trip home. As he was gazing into the grand ballroom, John ventured a remark. "Maybe we should come back here someday?" He looked questioningly at the glittering chandelier for a moment. There was no question about this. Jo's look echoed his feelings on the matter. No! There was no way that was going to happen!

They bid Albert and Karl a gracious farewell, got into John's car, and headed home. On the way out of town they passed the same bar Jo encountered Saturday night. John said nothing at first. Then he remembered something.

Reluctantly, meekly, he asked, "Josephine, how much of this do we *really* have to tell your father?"

"Probably not a lot." she ventured. "Nothing . . . ? Let me think."

They were silent then, each in their own thoughts until they got home.

35. TRUTH

John left Jo at her house and hurried to his own home. He told his parents everything that had happened concerning Pearce. While it was true Martha usually had her mind on social graces, and widely thought of as someone who only entertained trivial thoughts, she loved her son and was very concerned for him. Both she and Wallace assured John he had done the only thing possible in the situation that had been presented to him.

He felt they would react this way, but it was good to hear them say it.

"John, never doubt our love for you. You're a good man and we're proud you're our son," Wallace said. He needed to hear that too.

"We love you, John." Martha was in tears. Love for her only child ran deep.

There, they had said it. They loved him and had confirmed his innocence. Now he could believe it.

Jo went in and found everyone, especially her father, awaiting details of the trip. Alice noticed her new outfit, but Vivian noticed something else. Jo was happy. She had left them, morose and undone. The girl in front of her now was quite confident and at peace with herself. Obviously, the trip had done a great deal of good. Vivian wondered—had something else happened? She smiled.

Harrison didn't know what to think, so he decided to just listen. Sooner or later the details would come out. He could wait.

"Jo," Mary Alice greeted, unable to contain her excitement, "tell us about it. What was it like? What did you do?"

Jo was not about to tell anything until she had time to think. Figuring less would be more at the moment, she told them as little as possible.

"There's not much to tell, Jo said. "We had a good trip and enjoyed ourselves. I got this new outfit. Isn't it pretty?" she asked, changing the subject.

She could count on Billy Russell to tell a thing like it was. "Too modern for this town," he quipped. Everyone laughed at that observation.

"I think I need a nap," she said tiredly. I'll tell you more after I rest.

Okay?" She went upstairs quickly before there were any more questions from her family.

There was actually nothing to unpack. Her old clothes had been ruined physically and stained by terrible, harsh memories. She had left them in the trash at the Grayson, wanting no reminders. She hung up her new things and put on her favorite stay at home clothes. *Everybody should have an outfit like this,* she thought. Her plan was to just "rat" around the house, to be still a while, and tell as little as possible. Her parents needed to know what had happened. When she got enough courage, she would tell only what was needful in order to be honest about the trip. They had trusted her to go, and she would honor their trust with the truth.

John was another matter. Their relationship was a matter between a man and a woman. She did not have to tell them about that.

It was wonderful to be back in her room and surrounded by the safety of family. Delilah jumped up on the bed to be petted. Jo stroked the cat and found she had relaxed a little. Was it possible the cat was a giver? Everyone seemed to think of Delilah as a spoiled, narcissistic creature. That was true most of the time, but now Delilah was giving all she had, herself. Jo felt adoration in each purr, lick, and nudge of the cat's head. Maybe she had been a little too judgmental about the cat. *Maybe she had been wrong about other things as well,* she thought, as she drifted off to sleep.

John rested for a while at his home and knew the time had come. He went to Jo's house, where she met him at the door.

"Mom, Dad," she said, "We need to tell you something."

Harrison knew this would be what he had been waiting to hear.

John retold the events of the whole weekend to them. Jo assured them it was all true. Then they waited for the wrath that was sure to come.

Instead, Harrison began by saying, "John, thank you for taking care of Jo. Certainly, we never dreamed any of this would happen, neither did you. You didn't abandon her, you risked your life for her—and that was all you could do."

"I know you feel terrible for having to kill the man, but think for a moment. If you could redo that night, if you hadn't killed him, what would have happened?"

John knew the answer. "I have no doubt—he would have killed us."

"John, I've worked to save many lives. I've done everything in my power to make that happen, and do you know what I've learned?"

"No."

"I've learned the outcome, life or death, is not up to me. I have to try to save life. You had to try to stop Pearce from killing you. The bullet just happened to find a fatal place. John, the outcome, life or death, was determined before you walked into that room!"

John thanked Harrison and Vivian for understanding, and said he would be back another day. He needed to think some more, so he went to walk down by the creek that flowed just beyond the Fitzpatrick and Benton lands.

He picked some wild mint. He loved the way it perked his senses, always cool and refreshing. Strangely, this too was a habit he developed while living in Nashville. He would find a sprig in the strangest places. It always reminded him of home and brought him peace.

He looked at the way the sunlight reflected against the stream and was reminded of the way the gold chain on Jo's necklace had shimmered.

He thought more seriously for a moment and considered what Harrison had said. In the case of Pearce Davenport, life or death had been determined by the man's life style.

He knew Harrison was right; he would have to let go of this and get on with his life. But first, maybe he would just sit on the creek bank and enjoy being home. Again, he silently lifted a prayer of thanksgiving for mercy and forgiveness. He would finally have peace.

The scene in Nashville had been quite different that day. Two, young, police officers had gone to a fashionable house west of town, to the home of Pearce Davenport. It was quite early, so Richard Davenport, Pearce's father, answered the door himself.

"Good morning, Officers."

"Good morning, Sir. May we come in? I'm afraid we have some very bad news to deliver."

"Yes, please, come in."

"Mr. Davenport, we were called to a bar last night. I'm afraid there has been a shooting."

"And you want me to come down and bail Pearce out of jail," Richard interrupted. "Yes, I'll be right down." These words he spoke out of habit because Pearce had been in trouble several times before.

"No, Sir," replied Officer Cooper. "I'm afraid that's not it. There was a shooting, but we regret to inform you, Sir—Mr. Pearce Davenport has been killed."

Richard stood very still. He heard nothing at that point.

"Maybe you should sit down, Sir," suggested Officer West. They led the stunned man into his own living room.

By now Francis Davenport and their daughter came into the room. "What's this? What has happened?" she asked.

Richard spoke now, his voice showing unusual tension, "Frances, it's Pearce. They say he's been killed." The stunned man could not believe his own words.

Immediate wails and sobs broke the stillness of the room. When the room quieted a bit, the officers retold the events of the evening as factually and gently as possible.

Richard would not accept the story. "I don't believe any of this! Who did this?" he demanded.

"My son has been in and out of situations, that's true, but he would never kidnap a young woman or lay a trap to ambush a man as you suggest now."

"Mr. Davenport, we're telling you exactly what we saw and what is in the written report. I'm sure you'll have questions. If you'll come by the office tomorrow, we'll try to answer them. Again, Sir, Ma'am, Miss, we are terribly sorry for your loss." The officers left then, they had delivered the sad news.

The Davenports were left alone in their shock, grief, and unanswered questions. Disbelief turned first into acceptance, then acceptance into anger, and finally, anger became rage. Richard Davenport was not a man to take this quietly. He would find the man who killed his only son if it was the last thing he did!

Early Tuesday morning, Richard went to the police station to get the *real* facts about the killing of his son. Then, being an attorney himself, he went to see his friend Judge Blakely. He demanded a hearing, or an inquest, anything that would get to the truth.

Judge Blakely had been a longtime friend of the family and knew of some of the situations where Pearce had been involved. He had also heard the official side of this incident, and from an official position, a formal hearing was not needed.

Judge Blakely tried to comfort his friend, knowing the man to be distraught about his son. He could see his friend would not be quieted any other way, so he agreed to look further into the matter.

The next day Judge Blakely met with the family and said, "Richard, Francis, I grieve with you my friends, but I cannot in good conscience find wrong with anyone but Pearce. I'm sorry."

The heart-sick couple left the courthouse unreceptive of anything. Somberly, they went home to prepare for a funeral.

36. REAL SOUTHERN, REAL GOOD!

The next day Alice got up and came down to breakfast. It had been a little more than a week since she had been attacked. She still wore a bandage on her head, but it was smaller. She looked better too; her eyes were not as black today. She was almost as beautiful as ever.

She decided she could not wait to tell Jo her news and began in song like fashion, "I've got something to tell you, Jo." She stopped, gave a broad smile, and said, "Everett and I are getting married."

Jo squealed with surprise, genuinely happy for her sister, "How wonderful! When? Tell me everything, she begged".

"Late September. By then the weather will be cooler. You, of course will be my maid of honor. I'm thinking dark blue for the dresses. What do you think?"

"Yes, of course. The choice is yours," Jo said.

Alice continued with her plans, "Geri will also be a bridesmaid. We'll ask John and Avery to be groomsmen."

Thinking of Avery, Jo asked, "How is Avery? Will he be well by then?"

"Avery is doing much better and so is Geri. They'll be fine by then I'm sure."

Billy came down the stairs, and would have joined his sisters at the breakfast table. Seeing the time, he grabbed a sausage and biscuit and headed for the back door.

He paused long enough to say, "I'll be at the Benton's store all day today. Mr. Benton said he would be grateful for any time I could give him while Miss Elizabeth is taking care of Avery."

"We're proud of you for helping them," Vivian said. "I'm going with your father this morning when he checks on Avery. I'll see if there are other ways we can help."

Billy left then, his sisters and mom lingering over coffee.

Turning to Jo and Alice, Vivian said, "Maybe you girls could help at the store some, too." She knew she could count on them.

Though Vivian's family had enjoyed a life of ease, she had taught her children to be mindful of the needs of others. She knew from personal experience, most people just suffered in a private kind of hell without asking for help. She believed that a burning, after-life hell was real, but she also believed in a hell of the mind. She had been there!

Thanks to the care and concern of a friend, Vivian had been delivered from her unbearable anguish and was able to resume a full life of love and family. She doubted she would have survived physically or mentally if not for Corinne. Vivian owed her life to her. She would care for and comfort others as a way of repayment.

About the middle of June, everyone settled into a routine of helping out wherever needed. The healing of all wounds was progressing nicely, and eventually, all thoughts turned to the Fourth of July.

There would be a parade of fine pleasure and work horses, and matched teams of mules. Carriages would be washed clean for the event. Draped in red, white, and blue bunting, they would sparkle in the heat of the July sun.

Families would line Main Street to see their kindred in the parade. Little children would wave "Old Glory" without understanding the cost of the moment.

There would be a community picnic in the grassy commons area. The women folk of the town would all bring such delights as golden brown, crispy, fried chicken, homemade pickles, and sweet corn relish made from the roasting ears of an early crop.

Everyone wanted braggin' rights for the first, ripe tomato of the season. Vivian's father usually received that honor. Now it was Vivian who had the pleasure of slicing the ripe fruit in front of envious, old time farmers at the picnic, which would last until the last piece of blackberry pie was gone.

After eating, everyone would visit or play games under huge, cooling, shade trees. Horse shoes or napping seemed to be the favorite of old men and babies. Women just liked to talk and listen to each other, catching up on the latest unfolding drama in the lives of their friends and neighbors.

As the day grew too hot for comfort, families would go home to rest and cool for a while, sipping iced tea in the shade of their veranda. In the evening, they would come back to town for the highlight of the day, fireworks!

Little Charlie Miller sat eating his breakfast, a piece of his mama's fried chicken and a fresh, hot, buttermilk biscuit. He had been thinking about spending some of his money from running errands.

"Mama," he began, "When we get to the parade this mornin', could I go over to the general store and get me some jelly beans? Mr. Benton said he had a new flavor, some Cinnamon Hots, in honor of the Fourth of July. I been thinkin' I'd like to try some of them. Freddie Walters says they're real good, but I won't know for sure 'till I try them myself."

Ruth Miller looked at her son, amazed at how wonderfully good the boy was and said, "Charlie, I think you're right about that. Cinnamon Hots sound good to me, too."

She went on, "I'm not through cooking dinner for the picnic. The chicken and biscuits are ready, but I still need to make a dessert. Why don't you walk on over to the store and get your candy. You'll still have plenty of time to come home, and we can walk over together later."

"I think I will, Mama. Mr. Benton said the store would only be open until the parade starts."

Charlie went everywhere he could, barefooted. He liked the way soft, fine dirt and fat mud felt between his toes. If he squished them just right, he could make a fine, sharp footprint.

He went into the store and walked over to the display case where Mr. Benton had opened many different boxes of candy. It was truly a sight to behold for anyone with a sweet tooth and proved especially alluring to children.

There were suckers in beautiful colors, lemon drops, licorice twists, peppermint sticks, chocolate bars, and of course, jelly beans.

"Mr. Benton, could I get about two cents worth of lemon drops?" He knew his mama liked those. "And I've been wonderin' about the jelly beans. I think I want to try about a penny's worth of them Cinnamon Hots."

"I think you're gonna' like those, Charlie. If you don't, let me know, and I'll give you your money back."

That was something Charlie really liked about Mr. Matthew Benton. The good man wanted happy customers.

Matthew Benton was indeed a very good man, for long ago he had realized a truth about himself. He would live his life as though it were a gift, a joy to have been born, an absolute privilege to have walked even for a while on God's beautiful creation.

Matthew also thought a lot about Ruther Miller and her son, Charlie. He had often asked himself this question. If his own son, Avery, didn't have a daddy, who would look out for him? Would someone care if Elizabeth and Avery had enough? He hoped someone would. In any case, he was determined to watch out for Charlie and help Ruth in any way he could. He couldn't bring back Charlie's father, but he could treat the boy with compassion and maybe help teach him right from wrong. Matthew Benton was in good company. The whole town felt that way about Ruth and Charlie.

Charlie held the candy tightly in one hand as he went to the porch of the store. He decided to climb up on the wooden bench and watch the town a few minutes. There was always some activity, and today there was sure to be much preparation for the parade, picnic, and fireworks. He liked to see the way things came together. It would also give him a chance to try the Cinnamon Hots.

He popped one in his mouth. At first there was sweet as he bit down and started to chew. His mouth was instantly filled with sweet, juicy heat so delicious, he quickly popped in another. The jelly beans were so good! He would insist on his mama trying just one. If she didn't like them, she could have all the lemon drops. He continued to chew and quickly realized he needed water. He hadn't thought of that until now. Oh well, he'd be home soon.

He was sitting on the bench about ready to go home, when out of the corner of his eye, he saw something that troubled him.

"What 'cha doin', Mister?" he asked. No answer. "Hey, Mister, what are you doin' with Mr. Benton's apples?"

The gaunt, dirty man tried to ignore the child, but knew if he didn't give an answer, pretty soon the store keeper would come out to investigate.

"Be quiet, kid," the man hoarsely whispered. "I'm just lookin' for the best ones." He said this while stuffing three apples in his pockets.

"No you're not, Mister. You're stealin' them, and that's not right!

The man didn't know what to do. He knew he needed to run, but he was starving. He figured if he went to jail for theft, at least they would feed him.

Charlie got down from the bench and said, "Wait here a minute."

The man thought about putting the apples back. He also thought about running. But there was something about the way the child had spoken to him, more of a request. *Maybe—no,* he doubted anyone would have compassion on him. *Lord knows, he didn't deserve it.*

Charlie went inside the store and told Mr. Benton he wanted to buy three apples.

"Okay, Charlie; that will be six cents. Do you need anything else?"

"No, sir, I'll be gettin' home."

"Bye, Charlie."

Charlie returned to the man still waiting on the front porch. The little, barefooted angel took the man by the hand and said, "You come with me, Mister. My ma's a good cook, and she'll take good care of you."

The man could only stare from his hollow, sunken eyes at the boy. He had been living in the woods, eating almost nothing for over a month. From time to time he had managed to steal small amounts of food from farm houses, but he was so hungry now, and tired of the running and hiding.

All Mason Stoner could do was take the boy's hand and say, "Okay."

Charlie took Mason to Ruth's kitchen door and said, "Mama, I think this man needs our help."

Ruth had just taken a blueberry pie from the oven when she looked up. Seeing Mason's condition, she said, "Well, yes, Charlie. I believe he does. Won't you come in, Sir?"

"Yes, Ma'am, I believe I'd like that." He stepped in and immediately passed out on Ruth's kitchen floor.

"Quick, Charlie. Get a wet towel." The child obeyed.

Ruth wiped Mason's face until he revived from his exhaustion and hunger. She offered Mason water as he sat up.

"Thank you, Ma'am."

Do you feel strong enough to sit at the table and eat a bite?"

"Yes, Ma'am, and thank you," he said. He was truly grateful for their kindness.

That was the day Charlie and Ruth adopted Mason. Ruth had never done this before, but something told her this was right.

She observed the man, looking for anything in his demeanor, some indication of flaw in character or speech that would create a threat to her or Charlie. There was none.

She was sure this man had a story, and probably had lived a colorful life, but also, she was sure he had had some raisin' as the country folks would say. He seemed to know how to behave himself in the presence of a lady and a small child. She was also sure this man needed mercy.

Charlie and Ruth did not go to the picnic that year. Instead, they fed a stranger and gained a friend.

They could see the man needed more than food and shelter. He needed a home. In return for cutting firewood and doing other chores, Mason slept in the barn and ate with them. For the first time in his life, he felt at peace. He believed he could dig in here and maybe find some other odd jobs in town. He was ready to make a real change. This was his break, his chance. It was his time and he knew it.

The Crushing of Wild Mint

Little by little Mason allowed Ruth and Charlie to know him. He discovered something else; he learned to listen with his heart. They had expressed love and concern for a stranger. Surely, he could do as much for them.

He listened intently as Ruth shared with him the story of her late husband, and how she and little Charlie had come to this part of the country. The three lives would fit together harmoniously as they started their own story.

Back in town the parade was just about to start. John could hear the noise as he crossed the backyards on his way to see Avery. This meeting was long overdue. He was a bit apprehensive as he stepped up on the porch. John knocked on the frame of the screen door, and promptly Bowser growled. From inside, Avery called, "Come in, John. Come in and sit with me. I'm awfully bored. How am I supposed to be healing while the whole rest of the town is celebrating?"

John removed his hat as he entered. "Hello, Avery. How are you feeling?"

"Tolerable, I guess, considering."

John started again. "I've been meaning to see you, Avery. I wanted to give your wound a chance to heal. I've been thinking—and let me finish—I've got to say this. I'm truly sorry. I have not treated you or

Geri as I should have, the way a true friend should anyway, and I'm asking you to forgive me."

Avery knew the truth when he heard it, but this came as a total surprise, and he didn't know what to say at first.

He began, "I accept your apology." He could only extended his hand from a reclining position and went on, "I have to admit I haven't been always fair to you either."

John shook the hand offered in friendship. "Thank you, Avery. You're very gracious."

"Not at all, John, you would do the same for me. Let's just say it took us both a while to grow up."

"Now do me a favor. Mama was in a hurry and went over to the store without first bringing me anything to drink. I feel pretty good as long as I stay here on this couch, but getting up and down still hurts a bit. Could you go into the kitchen and get us some iced tea? Then, could you maybe stay a while and talk to me? With Mama, Geri, and Miss Corinne fussing over me, I'm gettin' a little crazy."

John laughed. "I can just imagine! Sure, be right back." He went to the icebox and got the cold drinks. On his way back to the living room, he overheard Avery tell Bowser, "Now you be nice!" The dog whined.

John gave Avery the drink and settled in a nearby rocker. They talked of many things, childhood memories, joys and sorrows of the past, hopes and plans for their futures.

A pleasant hour had passed when Elizabeth came home. "John, what a wonderful surprise to see you," she greeted. John stood.

"Miss Elizabeth, it's good to see you."

"Sit down, John, and visit with us a while. Matthew will be home in a bit."

"I can for only a minute, and then I need to get home. I'm taking Josephine to the parade." He winked at Avery.

He sat with his long time neighbors for a moment more, enjoying the comfort of being home and real friendship. He genuinely hated to leave, but excused himself.

Both Avery and Elizabeth asked him to visit often. They sincerely meant it.

The parade and picnic went as planned. It was as lively as any other Fourth. Children and dogs chased the fire truck as usual, begging for a ride. But this year, only John, Jo, and Billy Russell attended from their neighborhood.

Geri stayed with Avery, that was a given, and Mary Alice wouldn't think of going anywhere until she looked her best, so Everett stayed with her. They all settled for a picnic on the porch.

That night only Billy Russell went back to town for the fireworks display. He would sit with Freida Livingston. When it was over, he would walk her home. When they got to the rock quarry, he was sure she would let him kiss her. That was his plan anyway.

The brilliant colors of the fireworks, the bursting stars, and the screamers would be seen and heard for miles.

Anticipating the coming show, young couples all over town found their own spots in the mellowing darkness. Avery could only get to the porch, but he was with Geri. That's all that mattered.

The parents of the neighborhood settled in their annual spots on their back porches. As they sat watching the night time spectacle, they could not help but also see the lives of their families unfolding. On this evening, all was right with the world.

37. BILLY RUSSELL GOES TO THE DOGS

In Nashville that night, while the whole town celebrated a sparkling Fourth of July, a young woman made plans that would affect many lives.

"Mother, Daddy, I want to get out of this house for a few days. I think I would like to visit Celia Ann. Aunt Margaret and Uncle James won't mind. They've plenty of room, and I'm sure they'd like to know you're both alright under the circumstances."

Her father said nothing, staring blankly at the wall.

"I said I'd like to visit Aunt Margaret and Celia Ann tomorrow, and maybe I'll stay with them for two or three days!"

Jarred back to reality for the moment, her mother said, "Yes, go on. You shouldn't be here."

Pamela Jean couldn't believe what she now saw in her parents. They had been so happy, so outgoing, and now this was all that was left.

Everything in their lives had changed suddenly, violently. She needed some space and time away from them. They were biased, poisoned in their thinking, and she desperately needed to know the truth.

She had listened to their side of the story and was living with her own anguish. She had heard the other side too, but she found it almost impossible to believe the accusations. She needed to ask her own questions, find other sources, and figure it out for herself. The girl was tired of being told what to think, whom to hate.

Bitterness had overtaken her father like the onset of a disease. It had come on quickly, and now it held on tightly, eating away reason and humanity.

Her mother had a slightly different illness. Hers was a recurring loss of reality. The young woman felt if she didn't get out, she would become infected by the insidious diseases of grief and revenge.

Her family was wealthy enough to have help, someone to attend to the house and physically care for the needs of her parents. There really was no need for her to stay if she truly wanted to outrun the pervasive illnesses.

She would leave this house, and she wasn't sure if she ever wanted to come back. She loved her family, but felt she was suffocating. Truth, whatever it was, would be refreshing. She would look for the truth; she was sure it was there.

The fifth of July was going to be as hot as the Fourth had been. Billy Russell awakened early, dressed for the trip, and went to the kitchen. Vivian had breakfast ready. "Mom, you didn't have to cook. I could have had milk and a muffin or something."

"I know," she said, "but it may be longer than you think before dinner."

Vivian thought for a moment and asked, "I was wondering, Billy, could you do something for me when you pass the graveyard? Could you check on the rose bush I planted for Mama and Daddy?"

"I'll be glad to. Love you Mom, see you later."

"Love you too, Son. Take care of yourself."

Billy went next door to the Benton's. Matthew opened the back door and immediately attended to the business of the day. "Good morning, Billy. Come in. I've got a list of things we need from the wholesalers. It should be quite a load, but don't worry if you can't get it all in one trip. And Billy, we really do appreciate you making this trip for us."

"When you get to Lewisburg, just go east on Main Street. There's a big sign that says, "Justice Brothers Wholesale Goods". You can't miss it. They'll show you where everything is located and probably help you load it."

"Here's the key to the truck, and it's full of gas so you should be set. Do you have any questions?"

"No, Sir. I can't think of any."

"Well, have a good trip, Billy. I'll see you this afternoon at the store, and again, thank you."

He drove straight to Lewisburg. The trees along the way gave plenty of shade to an otherwise blistering road trip.

Finding the warehouse was not a problem either. He climbed out of the truck and went into the office. There, he told the clerk what he needed.

The wholesale company seemed to have everything any grocery or hardware store would ever need. Small packages of coffee, tea, flour and sugar were wrapped in large bales. These bales were stacked four to five high on wooden pallets. Small, farm tools hung from hooks around the walls while the larger implements stood in corners and in the fenced back lot area.

They went through the warehouse gathering everything on the list. Next, the clerk helped him load the small, flatbed truck, putting the heavier commodities on the outer sides and managing to get the small implements like hoes, rakes, shovels, and brooms to slide between the bales.

The Crushing of Wild Mint

To Billy's great satisfaction, everything fit perfectly except the supply of assorted candies. He tried wedging the large, oddly shaped bag between the bales with the tools, but it was too big to fit as it should. He knew it would just shake loose on the trip home and fly off the back of the truck.

"That's okay," he told the clerk. "I'll just put the sack in the cab of the truck."

He was pulling the bag down from between the bigger parcels, when a corner of the sack hung on a hoe blade and ripped. Before he could stop the hole, hundreds of jaw breakers in every color spilled out, rolling and bouncing onto the floor of the warehouse. He stood there with his mouth wide open. "Oh my stars!" he wailed. What had he done?

Laughter erupted behind him from the clerk's office. He turned, not feeling the least bit amused. The laughter continued. It was coming from two girls who were laughing so hard they were doubled over, crying.

"This is not funny!" he shouted.

"Oh, ha, ha, but it is *so* funny from here!"

Billy walked toward the girls shaking his head in disbelief of the situation. When he got to them he turned and looked at the truck, the bag hanging from it, and jaw breakers still rolling to various corners

223

of the warehouse. As he watched, one more jaw breaker escaped the bag.

It was too much for Billy. He turned to the girls and started laughing himself. "You're right." he said, "From here, it is hilarious!"

The girls, realizing the boy was truly in a mess, began to apologize.

"We're sorry," said one.

"Oh, yes, ha, ha, terribly," the other.

"I'll get a broom," offered the first.

"You need a bucket," the other girl quipped. That caused even more laughter as each went to find big brooms and buckets.

When the girls came back they remembered their manners.

"I am truly sorry for laughing," the first girl said. "I'm Celia Justice and this is Pamela Jean. My father and uncle own this place and you can believe us, we see this kind of thing a lot. That's why we have these big brooms.

"Yes," said Pamela. "We'll help you clean up the mess."

"I'd appreciate that," Billy said as he took a broom. "I'm Billy."

The girls extended their hands and smiled their sweetest smiles.

"So glad to meet you, Billy," each said.

That's when Billy realized these were two of the prettiest girls he'd ever seen. Celia had brown hair, "doe" eyes, and dimples, while Pamela Jean was fair, with blue eyes the color of morning glories, and lots of blond curls pulled back by a ribbon of pale blue.

They worked until every piece had been picked up. Then, they got another sack and repacked more jaw breakers. This time the sack went straight into the cab of the truck.

It was about noon so the girls asked Billy if he would like to get something to eat at the corner café, their treat. It was the least they could do for laughing they said.

"No, I'm sorry," he explained. "I should have been out of here an hour ago, but if you ever come to Caney, come over to the clinic. My dad works there. It's a small town and everyone knows us."

"What do I owe you for the spilled candy?"

"Nothing," Celia answered. "Like I said, it happens. Have a good trip home, Billy. Maybe we'll see you again on another trip."

"Maybe so," he agreed. "Thanks for the help."

He drove without incident back to the store and helped Matthew unload the truck. He was tired but remembered he needed to check on the rose at the graveyard before he went home.

He drove the truck back through town and stopped at the little iron fence. Leaving the truck by the side of the road, he walked through the fence gate and stopped at the graves of his grandparents, Faith and Thomas Morton.

It was always quiet and peaceful here, even so, he could hear dogs a long way off. *Probably chasing supper,* he thought. He had not eaten since breakfast.

The young rose was green and had a few buds and blooms. It was fine, but it would need water to get through the dry summer months ahead.

He sat for a moment quietly remembering how his grandfather had often taken him fishing and his grandmother had read stories to him from the Bible. Billy knew his life had been blessed for knowing these two dear souls. He sat for a moment, cherishing his memories.

A huge jack rabbit ran right in front of him as fast as he could go. Billy guessed the rabbit would not be anything's supper at that speed.

He could hear the rustle of leaves in the background. *Squirrels,* he thought, *foraging for supper.* Everything, it seemed, reminded him it was time to eat.

He was about to get up when from behind him he heard a low growl. Pitifully unprepared, he turned to face three, large, grisly looking dogs. Billy immediately knew he was in trouble. He froze, his mind quickly surveying the ground for anything he could find to use for a defense.

The biggest dog attacked, going for his chest. This one would knock down the prey. Billy realized he would only have seconds as his hand found a rock and swung, catching the dog's head just above the eye. Smarting with bright pain, the dog ran off into the woods in a constant yelping.

The other snarling mongrels began to edge to different sides, slowly circling him. They lunged at him, catching his clothes and hanging on until they tasted blood and meat. He fought them, kicking, beating, thrashing with the rock, but he was no match. They quickly pulled him down.

Billy kicked at the one on his leg. It wouldn't let go until he busted its head with the rock, pounding the dog until it was very still.

The last one had backed off to get a better hold. Circling, he prepared to attack again. As the dog lunged, Billy tried to defend his head with his left arm. The dog bit into the already torn flesh.

He knew the dog would kill him. These dogs were wild animals. They hunted in packs and knew how to take down anything they found.

This time Billy was ready with the rock and caught the dog just right. He pounded the dog's head until it let go. Licking Billy's blood from his foaming chops, he lumbered off into the woods, looking back only once as if he could take Billy; but the dog was dazed and he wasn't sure. Still growling, he disappeared into the nearby woods.

Billy too, was in a daze. He stood looking for others that might be lurking, waiting. He was trembling from pain and weak from fighting off the attack.

His clothes were bloody, his wounds were bleeding; he knew he needed to get help. Somehow he had to get back to the truck. He took a few steps and fell. He could feel nausea from exquisite pain begin to come over him. He could crawl to the truck if he had too, if only he did not pass out!

Fortunately, the truck was only a few yards away. He pulled himself into the driver's side and slumped across the seat just to rest a minute. The last thing he remembered was, "Dear Lord, help me! Let somebody find me."

At about three o'clock that afternoon, Pamela Jean had said good bye to her cousin. She had needed to be with young people. The visit, the whole day, had proven to be better than she thought possible. It was just what she had needed. She wanted to be alone now. Her parents thought she was staying with Celia, and Celia thought she was going on farther south. No one needed to know anything more right now.

She drove on through Chapel Hill, Tennessee, and was about to get to a smaller town when she noticed something. A truck was sitting on the side of the road with the door wide open. The legs of a man were hanging outside of the cab, his clothes bloody and torn.

That's strange, she thought. *Should she stop? It might be a trap. No, she could see a lot of blood. Someone was definitely hurt.*

She stopped her car and ran over to him, anxiety growing with each step. She recognized him at once. It was Billy. She ran over to her car to get the water jug that her Aunt Margret had insisted she take on her trip.

She splashed Billy's face with the cool water until he was revived a bit. He spoke one word, "Drive!"

She didn't know exactly where she was, what was ahead, or how far she would have to go. He had been going somewhere, so she would just continue in that direction. She drove as fast as she could into the little community of Caney.

Pamela did not have to look far. A large, plain sign three buildings ahead read "Clinic". She pulled the truck up and ran inside. "Help me, please," she cried. "There's somebody hurt out in the truck!"

Harrison quickly hurried outside. Then he saw Billy.

"Oh, Dear Lord, no!"

Adrenalin was already pumping wildly through the doctor. He knew he had to calm himself. That's easier said than done when it's your child who's in trouble. But he had too, really. He was the only doctor in town. Immediately he began to pray for wisdom on his part and healing for his son.

In about two seconds, Harrison went from stressed parent to trusting doctor. He scooped up the horribly mauled body of his son and dashed back into the clinic.

To his part-time assistant, Ruth Miller, he decisively gave orders. "Ruth, I need your help. Get the things I'll need to make an antiseptic poultice."

As the doctor assessed the worst injuries on Billy's arms, head and legs, he found the source of flowing blood, applied pressure, and stopped it. Stitches would be needed there. One of Billy's eyes was already bruising and swelling, but other than that, the doctor could see nothing except oozing, watery, bloody, puncture wounds from what he was sure were dog bites.

Harrison had seen this type of injury before. Some really bad cases in fact, but this, this was the worst he had ever seen. He knew from experience, after torn flesh and bleeding, infection from these animal bites was the enemy. Billy was in for a lot of suffering. The swelling at every puncture point could be awful.

The doctor meticulously cleaned every bite with an antiseptic wash. Then he applied a thick paste, creating a poultice that would act as disinfectant and have a soothing effect on the injuries. Over this, he would wrap a linen cloth.

He would also watch Billy for signs of rabies. He had some vaccine but hesitated to start the painful treatment if it was not necessary.

Harrison had done all he could for the moment. Remembering to breathe, he suddenly remembered the poor girl who had found his son.

Turning to her, he began a series of rapid questions. "Where did you find him? Do you know what happened?" He stopped a moment, shook his head in disapproval of himself, and started again. "I'm sorry.

I'm Doctor Windham and Billy is my son. I can't thank you enough for finding him and bringing him here." He paused again, thinking for a moment.

"I must to get word to my family, but I can't leave him. You've already done so much for him, but may I ask you to do one more thing? Would you please drive up this road about a mile—we're the big grey stone house on the left. You can't miss it. Go there, please, and tell my family what's happened."

She could not refuse his plea for help. Apart from the assistant, she was the only one there.

"Yes," she said, and quickly turned for the door, the waiting truck, and the unknown road.

Pamela Jean found the grey stone house and ran to the door. She pounded on it knowing she *had* to be heard.

Mary Alice opened the door. She could tell from the girl's expression there was trouble, but smiled as sweetly as always and said, "Hello, may I help you?"

"Billy's been hurt! Your dad sent me to get you! They're at the clinic!"

"Mama, Jo, hurry!" Alice called. "It's Billy! He's been hurt!"

Vivian threw her sewing down at once and ran for the truck with Alice and Pamela Jean. John was visiting Jo, so they raced for the car.

Harrison met them at the door of the clinic and said, "I think he'll be alright, but get ready for a shock." Harrison was standing in front of his son. He moved then, and all eyes fell on Billy.

His wounds had continued to swell. By now, huge bruises were coloring. Alice turned away in disgust. Jo blanched, stepping backward, John steady by her side. Vivian stood, disbelieving, turning her head side to side, her mind disputing what she saw. "No, no, no," she cried, "Oh please, Lord, no!" She went to him while Harrison tried to tell his family of Billy's condition.

After the initial shock settled, John turned to Pamela and asked, "Do you know what happened?" All eyes now rested on the young stranger in the room. All waited anxiously for the story.

Pamela retold everything she had seen. She paused then and said, "I'm *so* sorry all of this has happened. He really seems like such a nice person. I met him earlier today while visiting my cousin."

She then retold of their chance meeting in Lewisburg at her Aunt and Uncle's wholesale warehouse.

Harrison and Vivian realized no one in the room knew the girl, so Harrison introduced his family and John Wallace.

The girl spoke then, "I'm Pamela Jean," she paused a moment, "Pamela Jean—Justice."

It was getting dark now. Harrison and Vivian would stay with Billy Russell. It would be a long night. Even though the doctor had given something for pain, Billy mumbled something about "morning glories."

Pamela said, "Goodbye," and turned to leave. She suddenly remembered she was nowhere near her car in a town she did not know. "Could someone take me to my car? I left it by the graveyard, and I need to drive back to Lewisburg, tonight."

Jo spoke first, "We'll be glad to get your car."

Then Vivian, "But please, stay in our home. It's dark, and you don't know the area. You've done so much for us. Stay, and let us thank you properly."

Pamela hesitated only a moment. She knew she did not want to be alone on a dark road. That was needless danger and really stupid even for a seventeen year old.

She smiled then, "Thank you. If it's not an imposition, I'd like that."

They brought her car to the house where John bid everyone a goodnight and went home. Mary Alice and Jo got Pamela settled in the guest room, but sleep did not come for anyone for a very long time.

Pamela Jean was greatly relieved to have a place to stay for the night. She shivered again just thinking about how she had found Billy. The Windhams were a lovely family; she could see that from their manners and the concern they showed for each other. She considered herself lucky to have met them.

Billy had seemed so sweet, laughing with them at the jelly beans. Surely, the boy did not deserve any of this. She had to wonder what part luck had played in the events of the day. It was more like fate. She was supposed to meet this family. There was something else, too. She had met a man named John Wallace.

Mary Alice and Jo cooked a large breakfast and greeted Pamela with morning pleasantries. The sisters were torn between offering the right hospitality, which they knew their parents would want, and a real need to see Billy.

They were just about to sit at the table, when Pamela said, "Let's take this food to the clinic and check on Billy."

Jo and Alice looked at each other, then at Pamela. Mary Alice smiled and said, "Oh, thank you! We really wanted to go, but you're a guest, and we wanted to be gracious to you."

"No, I insist. If that was my brother, I would want to see him as soon as possible." She choked at saying this. "Besides, I can't eat a bite either—until I see that he's better."

They took the food to the clinic. Anxiety from the night before had been replaced by fatigue. Food and the girls were a welcome sight to Vivian and Harrison.

Billy opened his good eye, "Mom, Dad," he called.

"We're here, son." They all rushed to his side.

Billy searched each face. Love and relief were all he saw.

"You're going to be sore, Billy, but you'll live," the doctor said.

"Man, I hurt all over!"

"I expect so. You've got a lot of bites that are going to swell a bit more, and you're probably going to have some scars too," the doctor went on. "But you're going to be okay."

Harrison knew Billy could possibly need surgery at some point, but that would have to be much later. Billy was going to live. That was what mattered. The dogs could have killed him.

Billy looked again at each face. This time his sight rested on the stranger. He had met her somewhere, but where? Morphine had him a bit confused.

"Wait," he said, "I know you—morning glories." They laughed then. It was obvious; he had been talking about her blue eyes.

"No, I'm just Pamela Jean."

"Yeah, I remember." Billy was just that quickly sleeping again. They let him rest. He would need it for his recovery.

At last they were able to unwind enough to eat some breakfast. Slowly they settled into their usual southern manners, and in spite of the situation, enjoy Pamela's visit.

She thanked them again for their hospitality. They thanked her for Billy's life.

Pamela Jean decided she would go back to Lewisburg and visit

Celia Ann as she had told her parents. Alone on the road was no place for a young woman.

She had left home looking for answers. She had found more questions and something else, a renewed appreciation for her life. Horrible things sometimes happened in life, but life was meant to be lived, a forward movement. She intended to do that and to make the most of every day.

She could not stop the insanity that threatened her mother and father, but she would be there to try to help them through it. She could not know their instability would gang up on her, and coupled with her own grief, be almost too much for any one soul.

Before leaving the clinic, Harrison asked if there was anything she needed, anything at all they could do to repay her kindness. Her reply was, "No, of course not. But if you're ever in Nashville, please stay at the Greyson. Tell Albert at the desk to give you my family's reserved suite. He'll get word to my family that you're there. I'd like for you to meet my parents some time."

"Thank you, we'd like that as well. Jo and John will follow you to Lewisburg. We want to make sure you get back to your Aunt's home safely."

"Thank you," Pamela said, "That's very thoughtful. Goodbye."

Harrison stepped away from the cars as they pulled away and slowly out of sight.

Harrison, Vivian and Mary Alice went back to Billy. He was awake.

"Where is she? Where's Pamela," he asked.

Vivian gently reminded him, "She had to go home, son."

"But I didn't thank her. I didn't even say goodbye."

"You just rest, Billy. Later, when you're well, you can go to Nashville, and thank her in person."

"But I don't know where she lives. What if I can't find her?"

Vivian was a little relieved by now. "Billy, you've got the rest of your life to find her. That's time enough. Who knows, maybe she'll come back to Caney someday, or maybe you can find her through her cousin in Lewisburg."

Billy was fighting sleep again. "Yeah, that's what I'll do. I'll go look for morning glories. I'll find her," and he was asleep again.

Billy was in for a lot of pain, but he had been lucky; the dogs had not been rabid. The swelling gradually went away, and the wounds slowly began to heal.

Sometimes though, at night, he would be caught again in a nightmarish fight for his life. By day, he began carrying his gun when he went walking or fishing.

The one good thing that came from the day was meeting Pamela Jean. He knew his mom and dad were right. There would be a right time and place to find her and thank her properly. He would take time to heal and rehearse their meeting. A slow smile was on Billy Russell's face for many nights as he drifted off to sleep in thoughts of finding the beautiful girl behind the bluest eyes he had ever seen, pale blue eyes the color of morning glories.

38. THE DEAL

The summer rocked along without incident until about a week before Alice's wedding. Again, John had been walking and found himself in Vivian's garden. She was weeding with a vengeance.

"Something wrong, Vivian?" He asked.

"No, just working through something. Gardening helps you know."

"Vivian," he went on, "do you think Jo could care for me?"

"I don't know," she said, not wanting to get in the middle of something. She really did know, but he needed to hear this from Jo. "Why don't you go ask her? She's in the house."

He went in and said, "Jo, come walk with me. I want to talk to you about something."

He took her hand, and together they walked down to the grove of trees where they had played as children.

How will I begin, he thought?

Is this the day, she wondered?

Taking her hands in his, he faced her and took a chance. "Jo, I don't know when it happened, but I'm in love with you."

Jo seemed to go deaf for a moment. There was a noise in her head, strange clanging, bells maybe? She had waited so long for those words. *Was she dreaming?*

Realizing he had shocked her, he said it again. "Jo, I mean it. I love you with all of my heart." He found he liked the way it sounded. He saw the hope and disbelief in her eyes. He went on. "Will you marry me in the spring?"

She wanted to scream with delight, shout it from the tree tops! She had waited a lifetime for this to happen.

She couldn't help the long, slow, huge grin she felt creeping across her face. "Yes, John! I *will* marry you in the spring!!"

He pulled her close and kissed her with all the passion he had reserved for the moment. Neither of them wanted to break the embrace or the kiss. They could stand like this forever and just enjoy the magic that happens when hearts embrace.

The moment had already been too exquisite for both, but John had been thinking a lot about Jo since the trip to Nashville. He had been shopping, too.

To seal the deal he reached into his pocket, pulled out a beautiful ring with a very large, pillow shaped diamond, and placed it on her finger.

Jo could not believe her eyes or the whole day for that matter.

"Drat!" She knew it. She was going to cry! She didn't want to; she was happy beyond belief. John laughed and kissed her again. One of the biggest deals of John's life was set. She was going to be his, and that was all that mattered.

They agreed to wait and tell their families after Alice's wedding. That would be the gracious thing to do. It would also give them some time to adjust, to plan and dream the dreams that we all dream, the hopeful, positive, forward dreams of a good life.

39. WEDDING PREP

Four months had passed since Alice's birthday party. So much had happened that weekend. She didn't want to think about it. Sometimes though, you have to think about unpleasant, hurtful things in order to appreciate all you have.

She remembered her fears for her brother and sister and her own terror at being buried alive. She absent-mindedly felt for the scar on her forehead, just to make sure it was gone. The scar had faded, her face was unmarred, but the memory of that night would remain.

She thought of Everett. She had feared for his life, too. He had shot Dex, wounding him, and rescued her. She felt that was probably typical of Everett. She could count on him to do the right thing and temper it with mercy. She knew she was marrying a good man, and he loved her dearly. She was a lucky girl.

The Crushing of Wild Mint

It was time to put away the unfortunate chapter in her life and write a new one beginning with Everett.

Upstairs in her room she went over the list of things that needed to be finished before their wedding.

Alice had done the outward things to prepare for the celebration. The cake was being made downstairs today.

Vivian was seeing to that and the flowers, of course. The music was planned. Billy Russell had an arrangement with the owners of the restaurant in town to borrow their tables and chairs for the outside event. They would be perfect as they were, painted in creamy white, but would be even prettier dressed in soft white linen and decorated with candles and fresh flowers in shades of peach, burnt-orange, cream, and brown, with gray-green foliage and ribbon, perfect colors for late summer.

The arbor in Vivian's garden would serve as the focal point for the ceremony. It stood ready for any event year round. Vivian was meticulous about this and everything else in the garden. She felt the surrounding grounds of a home were indicative of the household itself.

Everyone's clothes, the dresses and suits, were ready. Everything seemed to be in order.

Alice had also prepared inwardly. She was ready to share everything Everett would ever face. She knew without a doubt, her love and acceptance of this good man had no limits. It was unconditional, unmovable, sure. There would be challenges, but they would go through everything together.

When thinking of a wedding, most people usually think of the bride, but Vivian had taught all three of her children that a wedding was a lot more than that. Though the celebration and ceremony of the wedding were for the couple, the preparation of the bride was for the groom. The bride should adorn herself, not just for the sake of being beautiful, for compliments and vanity, but beautiful especially for him. The groom should look at his bride and think he was a very blessed man to be marrying a woman of such excellence, finding exceptional beauty both inside and out.

The groom was to cherish his bride, holding her dearly, tenderly in his heart. He was to love her sacrificially, ". . . even as Christ loved and gave Himself for the church, His bride." (Paraphrased Ephesians 5:25 KJV)

Everett had already pledged this to her and proven to be there for her. She knew he would love her selflessly, sacrificially. He would seek to nurture and protect her all of his days.

They had talked about this many times; they were ready to be one. They would not smother each other's spirit, but each would seek to help the other develop into all God had created them to be and achieve.

She momentarily looked at Petey in his cage. "Petey," she asked, "would you sing at my wedding?" Petey had always been a confidant to Mary Alice. The little bird flexed his neck downward and slowly blinked assent. He knew Mary Alice loved him, of course he would sing. Had he not sung for her every day of his life? He loved her too.

She went to Jo's room. She needed to say some things to her sister.

"Jo saw the tears welling in Alice's eyes and said, "You are not going to cry. I forbid it! You are going to be a happy bride if it kills you!"

Mary Alice had to laugh at that remark. "I am happy!" she wailed.

Jo hugged her sister. "Look, you're not going to the moon. Everett lives less than a mile down the road. You're going to be very happy there. He loves you more than anything." Jo thought a moment more. What could she say to get Alice's mind off leaving?

She knew she shouldn't, but actually wanted to anyway. Now she had an excuse. "Can you keep a secret, Mary Alice? I mean *really* keep it? John will have a small fit if he finds out I've told."

"Yes. I can."

"You're not the only one leaving. John has proposed, and I've accepted. We'll be getting married in the spring."

Alice was elated at the news.

"Shh," Jo whispered. "Not a word to anyone! We're going to announce it after your wedding. Next week will be soon enough."

Alice thought a moment and said, "I guess all I need to say then is, Jo, I love you and I'll miss you."

"I love you too, Alice. But we'll be back and forth between the houses. There'll be no need to miss me or the family. You'll see." She hugged her sister then. "Here," giving Alice a handkerchief. "Dry your eyes now and be happy. Enjoy this moment in your life. Besides, you don't want a swollen face and red eyes tomorrow."

That sobered Mary Alice up quickly enough. Indeed, she did not want that!

Alice went downstairs to the kitchen. She said it was to check on the cake, but really it was just to keep busy.

Vivian and Everett's mom had everything well in hand, both were accomplished homemakers. Corinne was there too, helping out where ever she could. Where else would a best friend be? They had seen many happy occasions within this family, but none would top this wedding.

The layers of the square, white cake had been baked, and the largest was cooling on the cake platter. When finished, the cake would be a three tiered, visual delight, the layers graduated in size, the smallest on top. The confection would be frosted in pale, vanilla cream with a bouquet of fresh, creamy white, old fashioned roses placed on the top. More flowers would create a delicate cascade into a larger grouping of flowers at the base of the cake. Between each layer, there would be a glaze of lemon with bits of sweet coconut made from a recipe that was many generations old. If a wedding cake was supposed to represent the bride, this one was perfect. Both were a sweet delight to the senses!

Obviously, the women did not need Alice in the kitchen. She had much to learn there.

She decided to go next door and visit with her dearest friend, Geri. The broken arm had not slowed her down that much after the first couple of weeks, and now she was wearing a lighter cast.

Alice found Geri upstairs, trying in vain to find a successful way to hide her cast. She held a handful of daisies in various poses in front of her mirror. None worked.

Alice walked in and said jokingly, "No one is going to notice the cast you know. They're all going to be looking at that wild mass of red hair!"

Geri turned from the mirror, her serious face breaking into her most beautiful smile, genuinely thrilled to see her friend.

"Alice, I'm so glad you came!" She knew her friend well. Even if her hair was a mess, Alice would never have said it. She hugged her friend and said, "You're just jealous." In truth, Geri's hair was beautiful. So was Geri.

Standing beside each other, they caught a glimpse of themselves in the mirror. How long had they been friends? Forever! As far as Alice was concerned, Geri was her other sister. Geri thought of Alice in the same way.

Geri looked sad for a just a moment.

"Don't you dare cry," Alice said. "Nothing will change. You're still going to think of things to get into, and knowing me, I'll still go along with them. You'll always be my best friend, Geri." She hugged her again.

Changing the subject, Alice asked, "Are you happy with your dress?"

"It's beautiful."

Jo's and Geri's dresses were not blue. Alice had decided on a delicate shade of brown, an artful work of silk and lace similar to hers, but shorter.

Alice would wear a dress of ivory tulle and lace over satin. The bodice featured a portrait neckline, the lace extending to create short, cap sleeves. A sash of champagne colored satin encircled the waist. The beautiful fabrics of lace, tulle and satin were styled to fall into a softly flowing skirt, the back a little longer, creating a slight train.

Jo would wear her lustrous, golden brown hair up. Geri's would be free and flowing. Both girls would be so beautiful that Alice couldn't help but wonder if anyone would notice the bride. No matter, she wouldn't have it any other way.

The girls had agreed to meet in Vivian's flower garden to choose the flowers for their bouquets. They would pick them today, put them in water, and before the ceremony, Vivian would tie them with ribbon.

They choose peach and white roses, bittersweet and mock orange blossoms for Jo's and Geri's bouquets.

Alice would carry a simple bouquet of creamy white roses with golden centers. These flowers were not only heirloom gifts from her grandfather Thomas' garden, but also Alice's favorite. Tied with wide, ivory satin ribbon, the bouquet would be perfect.

That evening, everyone who had anything to do with the wedding gathered at the Windham home to go over the plans for the service. John's mother, Martha, was in charge of the rehearsal, no worries there. This woman had been to more than her share of formal affairs. She planned her life around all of the area's social events and enjoyed every one of them.

"The key to a successful event," she said, "is always the same. Have fun and plan ahead so each guest is glad he or she came."

Martha was a great, practical presence. She had the knowledge and power to make things happen, and everyone had great confidence in the woman. All just did as they were told, with no friendly "help" being offered or solicited.

Everett's parents gave a reception in honor of the couple at their home after the rehearsal.

A wonderful meal of roast beef and late summer vegetables was enjoyed. The parents and the minister lingered with desserts of fresh apple pie and coffee in the dining room, while the younger people gathered on the welcoming veranda of the farmhouse. Small, lighted candles twinkled to create a more intimate atmosphere.

The young friends gathered in couples now, except for Billy Russell. He was as a little brother to them all, and content just to be part of a group of friends who cared so much about each other.

Everett was the host tonight, and as such, he stood and began. He had something to say; it was what everyone was already thinking.

To his dear friends he said, "First, I want you all to know how much I love Mary Alice. You already know that, but I wanted to say it in front of you, our dearest friends.

Then, turning to look at Mary Alice, "I don't know what's ahead for us, but I will always love you just as I do at this moment, and if we're very lucky, we'll grow old together."

Alice's heart was full; life was so very sweet. She smiled and agreed, "We will!" Everyone there knew Everett meant every word he had just said. He was an uncommon man of sincere, truthful speech.

He continued, "Next, Alice and I want each of *you* to know that we love you. We cherish the time of growing up with you and pray that our friendships only grow stronger."

He raised his tea glass then and said, "To dear friends. May our lives be good and beautiful, our futures blessed in every way. May we always hold dear our friendships and cherished memories."

As the light of early evening faded, it was as if a quiet kind of glow settled upon each face. Hopes for their futures, peace for settled situations, and joy for the occasion was reflected one to the other. Sounds of laughter and soft voices trailed into the soft September night, the perfect end to a late summer day.

40. BITTERSWEET

Late in September on the stair landing of a fine, old, grey stone home stood a young bride. Mary Alice wore her grandmother's pearl and diamond earrings, Everett's pearl chocker with the delicate aquamarine, and a beautiful satin and lace gown.

Her mother and sister had arranged her hair by gathering it in soft curls, low on the nape her neck and to one side, allowing a few tendrils to escape around her face. Flowers and a sheer, full length veil of lace and tulle were pinned into her hair, the veil, a companion piece to her dress. She carried the faith of her father and a bouquet of roses from her mother's garden.

She stood there thinking, I *must not cry, I'll ruin my face*. She couldn't help it. Her heart was set on marrying Everett, but her family stood at the foot of the stairs looking up at her.

There were so many mixed emotions in the room. Especially in families where love abounds, there comes a time when it is recognized, everything is about to change. This was their moment.

Mary Alice spoke to each one. "Josephine, you're beautiful in every way. Be sweet to John, that's the key." She winked and thought a moment. "Oh, and please, please, watch out for Petey while I'm gone. Don't let Delilah scare him."

To Billy Russell she smiled and asked, "Who will keep you in line?"

"Mom, Dad"... her chin quivered, tears were on the way, threatening a spill.

Harrison walked forward to take his daughter's arm. "We love you too, Mary Alice. We'll be here if you need us." Then he kissed her.

Her mom joined them and said, "Today is only the beginning, Mary Alice. You need to enjoy it with Everett." She looked at Harrison as she went on. "The trust you two share today will grow and serve you well in the days to come. Young love is exciting, but mature love grows deeper every day." Vivian paused to smile before she continued her reassurance, "Alice, when it's right, and this is, it only gets better."

She kissed her daughter then and walked on to her place as the Mother of the bride on the arm of her son.

A small ensemble of violin, cello, and harp played as Harrison escorted Mary Alice to the garden. There, under an arbor of late vines and flowers stood Everett, waiting for Harrison to place Alice's hand in his. He took her hand and was instantly overcome with emotion; he realized he had never really seen beauty before that moment, and, *she was his.*

Alice had been thinking about how much she would miss her family. Upon seeing Everett waiting for her under the arbor, her only thought was, *this beautiful man is waiting for me!* She wanted to be his more anything. *If she could only slow time,* she thought. The ceremony was moving too fast. She wanted to remember this moment, for it was the moment she fully trusted Everett with her heart. She smiled as she took his hand. Confidence was on each face.

The bride and groom each knew what they were getting in this union. With Alice, Everett was getting the embodiment of kindness and understanding, a garden for his soul, fertile ground for his hopes and dreams. She would tend that garden, filling in any broken place, praying for him daily. She was a vessel of faith.

In Everett, Mary Alice would find strength, a shield against the harshness of life, shade from the heat of the day. In that shade, she would find peace. Encouraged to grow, her life would blossom and spread, a blessing to those around her.

Each would be as a priest to the other as the Levitical priests of old. Priests, who daily offered prayers for the sins of the people while tending a glowing censer. Mary Alice and Everett would continually offer prayers on behalf of each other, their prayers too, rising as smoke in a censer. Every heart's cry would be heard.

The elderly minister began, "Dearly Beloved," but after that, he departed from the usual theme of love, for this was no usual preacher.

Reverend Martin had been a pastor in the community for at least thirty years. He came to the community in mid life and carefully attended to the needs his flock. He had watched many grow old and go to their final reward. He had also christened many babies and witnessed their lives unfold as young plants before the sun.

Reverend Martin opened the service using verses from Galatians 5:13 and 6:2. . . . "By love serve one another," and . . . "bear ye one another's burdens." He closed with the example of Christ as servant.

Having been married for over fifty years, he knew love would change and grow. At first there would be excitement from all the first things of life, the thrill, the newness of being a couple. But the new family would also be challenged in more ways than they could imagine now. Love would get them started, but gratitude, forgiveness and humility, an attitude of servanthood, would sustain them.

The old minister then led them through their vows of commitment. As Everett placed a delicately carved circle of gold and diamonds on Alice's finger, he spoke from his heart a poem, the same poem he had memorized for her so many years ago.

He began, "Mary Alice, you never need to hurry, I will wait for you."

"As long as a summer's garden

Releases tender perfume,

I will wait for you.

As sure as honey grows sweet,

Amber in the tree,

I will wait for you.

You will not wait long

For me,

I shall run to you.

Neither will I wait long—

For you will fly to my side.

As long as the rain falls,

As sure as a Whippoorwill calls,

I will always love you—

And I will wait for you."

The wedding and reception that followed had been perfect, exactly what Alice and Everett had wanted. The flowers, food, and music, everything fit together to compliment and represent the couple.

They changed into traveling clothes for a honeymoon on the Atlantic Coast. She chose a navy suit, he gray. In a hail of rice and good wishes, they left the beauty and protection of the garden carrying the love of family and friends.

Settling into the car that would take them into the first chapter of their life together Everett asked, "Are you ready, Mrs. Mackenzie?"

"Yes," she said. Alice knew her mother was right about being with Everett. She would just enjoy this moment in time.

She turned to say goodbye, and threw her lovely bouquet to the waiting hands of her sister. Jo searched for John across the crowd. Finding him, he smiled and nodded back at her.

Everett was taking Mary Alice east. He wanted her to see the Atlantic Ocean and planned to take his time comparing the color of her eyes to the color of the sea.

Like most husbands, he would spend the rest of his life trying to understand the inner workings of her mind and heart. At some point he would finally understand what his own father had told him on this wedding day.

"Son, women are a mystery." Everett had laughed!

41. JUST SAY GOODNIGHT

The bridal couple left then, stepping into their own adventure, but that's another story.

The reception for them continued into early darkness. It was late September, and the days were growing shorter. Guests continued to enjoy both the food and music, and general atmosphere of the setting. It also gave them a chance to graciously thank Harrison and Vivian for their hospitality and say, "Goodnight."

Geri looked as beautiful as ever, always smiling, beaming. And why not, did she not see pure adulation in the eyes of Avery? He pulled her closer to him as they danced. He found the spot just under her ear and kissed it. She giggled and blushed. *Life could be absolutely thrilling at times,* she thought.

Josephine had caught the bouquet, and with that, she winked at John. That was his cue. He dodged couples and small children until he stood beside Jo.

Looking at her, he remembered the rose satin dress and how they had danced. That had been the start. She had been both vulnerable and beautiful that night, quite alluring as he remembered.

"Jo," he said. It was the way he said her name. "Jo, brown silk and lace are not meant for standing in the shadows." He thought a moment more and whispered, "Well, maybe they are," as he pulled her out of the crowd and into the soft candlelight of the nearby patio. She looked very surprised, but very pleased!

He kissed her, taking his time. The mood of the whole evening had been very romantic. Everything had suggested intimacy. To John, moments this beautiful, this perfect, were rare in life and shouldn't be wasted or rushed.

Jo returned the kiss, allowing her arms to slip beneath his jacket in their embrace. She loved the way his white shirt felt under her hands, but more than that, she loved the way this moment felt, steady and sure.

They could have stayed there a very long time, but another couple had the same idea. The music started again, and John said, "Let's dance, Jo." He led her to an empty spot to enjoy a few moments of being close there.

Guests were beginning to excuse themselves now; it was getting later, the crowd thinning.

Jo led John around to the back porch. They could say goodnight there; that would be more private.

They stood talking, making plans, sharing hopes for the future, when John remembered something. He reached into the pocket of his jacket and found Jo's engagement ring. "Here," he said. Finding her hand, he put the ring on her finger to stay this time. "We can tell everybody now; it's official!"

About that time, Avery and Geri walked around to the back of the house, hand in hand. They would cut through the yard and be on Geri's front porch in about two minutes. They would sit there, gazing at each other, until Corinne told Avery it was time to go home.

"Avery!" John called, "Geri!" They came over to the porch already knowing, probably, what he was going to say. Even in dim light, Jo was radiant with joy.

"Avery, Geri, we want you to be the first to know. Jo and I are getting married in the spring."

Too late, Geri had already told Avery what Alice made her promise to keep a secret. "Act surprised," she had said. He remembered.

Stepping up onto the porch, Avery extended his hand to John. "Well congratulations!" he said, and he meant it.

John accepted his hand and replied, "Thank you." He also sincerely meant the words he said.

Both young men had endured much in the last few months. They had tried to keep their distance through the years, but life has a way making you see the sufferings of others. There had been many changes in the young people that spring. The string of dark events, the brutality and fear, had brought maturity and gratitude to all. Old hostilities gave way to trust and real friendship.

Bowser had been dozing under the nearby bushes on paws extended. He perked up his head at this turn of events. *Well*, he thought. *What was this? It was about time! Could he have been wrong about John? Not a chance!* Bowser decided he would remain cautiously hopeful. It might work. He would hold off any conclusions until he had further proof of a "new" John.

Another thought for Bowser—*Too bad, he was gonna' miss terrifying John.* The dog rather enjoyed that. He put his head down again and closed his eyes, secure in the knowledge it would work out either way. He snorted in his glee and went back to sleep.

"We're very happy for you both," Geri said.

"Thank you," they replied.

Avery and Geri said goodnight and walked on toward the grove of trees. In another minute they would pass the picket fence then settle in the wicker swing on the Judge's front porch.

Josephine settled in her mother's rocker, John in Harrison's. Her father came through the screen door of the kitchen. He was there to say goodnight to John, and in his own way, gently suggest to him it was time to go home.

Jo and John got the message.

He kissed her goodnight, but his look said so much more.

She whispered, "Goodnight," with a look of longing and pleasure on her face. They could give up this night only because they knew there were so many more in their future.

The screen door screeched as usual when Jo went through it, as if in closing the whole day.

42. WAKE UP AND GO TO BED!

That's when the old woman woke up. It was the screen door. She had heard it screech as Harrison came to join her in their afternoon ritual. He sat in the same chair John had sat in all those years before.

Vivian had slept through the early afternoon in her chair as usual, waiting for Harrison to come home. Harrison, long retired now, would go to town every day and visit with neighbors on his way back home. He was always back by supper time.

Harrison would allow Vivian all day for her garden, but the evenings he reserved for himself. There could never be enough time for this woman. He loved her more now than the night they had eloped. She felt the same way about him.

"Are you ready for supper?" she asked. "I cooked a mess of green beans today."

"I know. I tasted them on the stove when I came through."

"Let's go in," Vivian said, "I'll fix you some tea and we can eat."

They sat at the kitchen table now. The big, beautiful, dining table had seemed empty when Alice, Jo, and Billy moved out.

The smaller table felt right somehow, complete, just the two of them. They had been given so much more than material wealth, for they also had the blessings of long life, health, and the love of a friend. Life was still very rich and good!

As they sat enjoying the garden's bounty, they grew silent, each in their own memories.

Harrison looked at his still youthful, beautiful wife, thought of his children and grandchildren, and counted his blessings.

Vivian counted her blessings too. But slowly as she savored her tea, traces of memories began to stir. She remembered their little Sam, Jr. and now understood his death had happened to Harrison as well, not just to her. She knew tragedy had taken not only the child, but all three had been its victims.

She could not remember when, but at some point, she had stopped asking the "why" question. Knowing why would not change anything. There were simply some things in life you had to accept and go on. Some things would never be understood; no one had to be at fault or to blame. A cleansing wash came over her, freeing her for other memories.

She recalled little Charlie and how he grew into the good man his mama, Ruth, had reared him to be.

She remembered the day Mason walked into town, the things he had gone through. Somehow Charlie had known what the man needed. Most folks would have just looked the other way. It was a rare person who would take in a stranger the way Ruth and Charlie had.

These were all memories and stories for another day. "Tomorrow," she sighed, "Tomorrow will be soon enough."

Harrison asked if there was any mint for his tea. He had come to love the aroma as much as Vivian did.

Putting a sprig in his glass, she thought about how in every life there is a sprig of mint, a measure of hope. It is in the crushing of our hope that we find what we are made of, what we are capable of doing, and the person we have become.

The expression of our mint would not happen if not for the crush, she reasoned. That could be as light as a touch, like the brush of a leaf, or it could be devastating, as in the crushing of the stem. The fragrance would be proportionate to the crush. As in life, we are touched by situations, sometimes harshly.

She continued to reason. We are attacked by struggles and worries in life. Sometimes it feels like we will not get through situations. Our mint, our hope, breaks! The despair, the hurt or heartbreak we feel, is the crush. It is the crush that releases our fragrance, how we will deal with things. Will it be the sweet fragrance of love, selflessness, and forgiveness she wondered, as in the lives of Corinne, Geri and Avery, or bitterness to the detriment of others, as it had been with Dexter, Farley and Pearce?

Then she realized something else, the healing love of Christ, expressed through the love and concern of a friend, had literally saved her life. It had pulled her through the darkest most desperate hours and given her new hope. That same love would continue, sufficient to heal any crush, any circumstance, or situation. It had healed her, and she had seen that love heal the lives of others.

And when they were crushed, no matter which fragrance was released, that same redeeming love was there for everyone, patiently waiting to minister, to heal or forgive as needed. Always, the humble spirit of Christ stands ready, waiting for us to allow Him fellowship through a daily walk and reliance on Him.

Vivian had been given the gracious gift of time. She had grown to treasure that close relationship more each day because she had found God to be faithful; she could trust Him with the most precious things in her life. The result, her life had been good, rich and full.

Just then, Dee Dee scratched at the door, her claws hanging on the screen. Meowing, reminding Harrison she had not had supper. As he stood to feed her, he up-ended his tea glass, rattling the last bits of ice, the clunk, chink sounds breaking Vivian's thoughts.

Her mind just as quickly jumped to Henry Milton. *What had that man been thinking?!* She could only shake her head at that memory. Did he really believe he could get away with taking the money? She instantly remembered what his thoughtless lack of regard for others, his selfishness, had brought on her family. That one critical moment had changed all their lives.

Everyone involved had forgiven him, including Vivian. No one had ever spoken of the theft again. To his credit, Henry had lived up to John's aspirations for him. He had become the man John and Harrison knew he could be. It was too easy to judge; she would quit!

She and Harrison cleared the table together. They did most things together it seemed; sometimes it took both of them to get a job done. That was good in a way since they now had all the time in the world.

Another day had come to a close. They would climb the stairs together, remembering the beautiful events of life, the weddings, births, their anniversary, and friends. Tomorrow would be another day, and they could replay the whole thing again. Harrison kissed her goodnight as he had on their wedding night, another beautiful memory. Each looked to the other as they had then. They would ever be the same.

Harrison was asleep as soon as he turned over in the bed. Vivian was alone in her thoughts for tomorrow. She would go barefoot to the porch, just as her father had done. This time she would carefully hold the screen door as it closed. . . . . .

EPILOGUE

And that's what happened in the town where nothing ever happens. Things settled. Everything went back to the way it was, more or less. It would be a long time before conditions were right for another storm. On the other hand, the people involved had been changed for life. The altering of their lives would in turn change the town in many ways, but that too, is another story.

We all think we know what we would do in a given situation. The truth is, no one knows for sure until that moment comes. Henry Milton did not get up one morning and decide to rob the bank. Opportunity presented itself, and Henry went for it.

It's easy to judge, but before you judge Henry too critically, ask yourself this; what would you do if you had the key to the bank in one hand and the combination to the safe in the other?

CPSIA information can be obtained at www.ICGtesting.com
Printed in the USA
LVOW122329200912

299616LV00002B/3/P